IN THE SAN

OACE AL MANSUR

In the San, by Oace Al Mansur © 2021
ISBN: 978-1-7353273-4-1

ACKNOWLEDGEMENTS

I would like to acknowledge anybody that listened while I ranted about this book I was working on, or how I was so excited about this new scholar I found out about that revealed all the information I needed to piece together a chapter in my story that came out of imaginative thinking. Although sometimes if felt like my ancestors were whispering visions into my consciousness, while my pen painted pictures of action-packed scenes. Maybe these weren't just characters in a book but more like untold cries of the many ancestors we lost connection with due to being a people stripped of any cultural identity.

To my mother that encouraged me and listened to my boring thesis on how important it is to depict black people's immaculate accomplishments prior, post and present day to slavery.

To everyone I briefly described my manuscript to and responded "I can't wait to read it".

To my constituents that read parts of my story and gave me feedback. Thank you.

To my fellow authors and writers that understand the loneliness that goes into being so consumed into your writing you become trapped in your own thoughts for hours, and thousands of words later you realize you're not the same person when inside your penmanship. You activate a different part of the brain that leads you to different skills within yourself you never even knew you had; let's keep writing. Let the fact that some may not listen when we talk be the fuel to keep us writing out our legacy that will last forever.

To my beautiful children, God willing you will read this book in your lifetime, I pray it gives you some type of guidance, I pray you can get a lesson out of it and use it in your life to find purpose.

Contents

PREFACE

This book came out of an idea I had sitting in the County jail cell like most of our true revolutionaries found themselves. The time for a person to clear his thoughts to find his or her self. I sat there reading literature, I sat there like George Jackson in solitary confinement imagining being able to talk to the authors and revolutionaries I revered even though I had no idea why.

Why did I idolize (Malik El hajj Shabazz) Malcolm X? Why did I get mesmerized by J.A. Rogers? Why did I become captivated by the genius mind of Ivan van Sertima? Why did I fall in love with Carter G Woodson's analogies? Why did I embrace the philosophy of Marcus Garvey? How did Anthony Browder Nile Valley Civilizations change my imagination? The greatness of these scholars as writers and leaders took me to a place away from the fictitious lies, I had been taught.

The redirection of purpose blossomed into embracing my thought process and stop asking why. The whys turned into me moving my pen from a proven self-educated experience and nobody can take that from me, not even the prison industry. Prison helped me learn patience, humility, and I learned how to channel my focus to be able to retain information. The same way Malcolm X and George Jackson educated themselves about everything from history, political science, mathematics, and sociology. I took their autobiographies close to my heart.

It made me realize that life is so short, we must read about other people's lives to seek guidance as we travel through life. I didn't want to waste any more time. If this truly was my purpose, I was determined to challenge myself until I found that purpose. I wanted to capture the moment and become who I was destined to be.

So, I re-read the pre and post-chattel slavery research, scattered chapters I had the descriptions of characters from the Haitian revolution the greatest revolution known to mankind. The precautions taken by slave masters in different countries because of the resistance to chattel slavery during the years leading up to Haiti's independence were real. I placed myself in a time when I never had been physically, I had to feel a time-lapse in between the forgotten stories and folktales of the past.

Haitian history deserves more recognition in middle and high school education in lower-class areas across America. If I fought bravely against oppression in a time of Revolution, how would I feel? What would I do? How would it affect the future of the oppressed? No, instead this story will prove there is no future in oppression.

The process and imaginative writing during a time in history are to the creative's advantage. The thrill of knowing the character's personality then sharing it with the reader; I feel it's the soul that writes, while the flesh only follows. Now here I am, entangled in my data with a story that will shed light on the Haitian impact around the world and into the Caribbean.

The victorious rebellion, this story is guaranteed to help the reader appreciate the true meaning of resistance. It will show the Haitian people were willing to die before being oppressed any longer. It shows the cost of freedom comes at a high price. It forces you to make the utmost sacrifice in hopes those after you will be free or gladly die just the same. So many martyrs went nameless from the Gullah swamps all the way to the tides of the most remote tropical islands in the clear blue waters of the Atlantic.

I will take you on a tour through generations that fought in the revolutionary war to another generation of black ex-slaves that fought for the same cause with even greater odds against them. A harsh battle against three countries with greedy intentions all trying to lay claim to the benefits of the land. All to no avail. I feel obligated to use illustration based on true events to share our ancestor's stories all the way across the Atlantic.

Just as history has King Author, Leunitis, Napoleon, General Robert E. Lee, Christopher Columbus, Amerigo, and the writers of *The Declaration of Independence,* we also have a fight for independence against oppression that deserves a deeper look.

All my life I have been on a continuous fight to find freedom within myself as a man without an understanding of a system that was formed to oppress me. I was a victim of being oppressed intellectually and systematically. And believe me, this is no pity, my life was real. The public school system failed me. I was surrounded by guidance counselors that couldn't relate to my situation of a single-parent home. I saw my friends die violently; this resorted to my neighborhood collecting weapons in a rebellion which manifested into self-hatred because I had no idea who the real enemy was but somehow the opposition looked like me.

The feelings of not having a father for guidance in life could have played a part in one being so lost. Lost to the point of accepting an inferior way of thinking based on lack of knowledge and understanding. I did not know myself, therefore, how could I possibly be a productive citizen in a society that was full of injustices that I at the time was unaware of.

My intellect had been oppressed, however throughout this oppression, I still was eager to learn. I needed direction and most of the ideas, slang, and topics came from what most of the young black generations are influenced by something called hip hop culture. Not understanding at that time one of the elements of hip hop culture is knowledge. Looking back, I know now this was the reason I would skip all my classes except history, on occasion sitting front row and hoping to learn something more than the history of plantation slavery and the Martin Luther King speech or the underground railroad.

I had a selective taste for something, what that something was I had no idea. I needed my brain to be stimulated like when I listened to Nas, dead prez, Cormega, or AZ. I found out the education I needed I wasn't getting. I wasn't interested in the way the curriculum seemed to be hiding something. I needed to seek for myself and self-educate.

The public school system never taught us what Carter G Woodson said, "There are two kinds of education, the one a person is taught and one a person teaches themselves."

I never knew anything about intellectual property but now I'm trying to perfect my craft with a new appreciation for original ideas. I'm just trying to capture what hasn't received the proper historical respect. We know history will always put everything in perspective and one must be honest about their perception of history. In The San' is the Haitian revolution through a soldier's eyes. Not only his eyes but his emotions, his journey, the mystical meaning behind his purpose during the time of political colonialism and guerrilla warfare. The obvious issue of racism plays a factor while Toussaint and Dessalines get glorified which is well deserved for the great leaders and revolutionaries they will always be.

In The San gives you the raw intense passion of the soldier that took up arms with those great men, travel with me on the voyage of perfect bloody rebellion in the struggle to survive as a soldier in the greatest ex-slave liberation in history and beyond. The grips of oppression did not stop at the coast of San Domingo. The path set out for equality will go far past the Caribbean islands into new lands with new greedy tyrants trying to get their fortune at the cost of inhumane conditions.

"There is no longer any hope for justice other than bloody rebellion,"

-Frederick Douglass

(At the anniversary Convention of the anti-slavery society in Salem Ohio.)

PROLOGUE

"Peter," Mr. Collins yelled out. "Make sure you watch that Nigger." Mr. Collins's voice was filled with hatred towards Abram.

Peter Held the Kentucky rifle to his temple commanding him to get on his knees. Peter loved anything violent or warlike, he was anxious to get back to the days of killing and the adrenaline rush of military conflict. He missed being side by side with his old comrade, who happened to be Mr. Collins's father. So many things about Mr. Collins reminded Peter of his father and he took full advantage. Abram's sweat soaked the long-barreled rifle, his heartbeat echoed through his body as he stared at Mr. Collins pressing the double-edged dagger to Sarah's throat. Blood dripped from the blade onto the hay of the barn

"Don't scream, you stupid nigger!" Mr. Collins said as he forced himself inside her. "Make sure he's watching Peter; this is the only way they will learn."

His hands were wrapped around her neck as he continued to violate her.

A young and confused Scott had snuck out of the house and watched his father and Peter transform into savages right before his eyes. He barely recognized his own father. He was more like a monster now. A wretched beast abusing two helpless people. Peter Stood still; focused on Abram, praying he will make a sudden move so we can blow his brains out. Sarah cried out loud to God.

"Shut up!" Mr. Collins yelled as he released himself inside of her womb and on her chest. Mr. Collins got to his feet, pointed at Abram, and said "I see how you look at her. I see how y'all look into each other's eyes on my fields. I know you want her to be your wife and have yer kids. Hell, I want you to have kids. I need more stock."

Mr. Collins chuckles as Peter laughed and his sarcasm

"But I own both of y'all and don't you ever forget that, Abram."

Abram's heart burned with fury; rage took over his soul as he stared into Mr. Collins's eyes. He tried to pray and for the first time, he didn't know who to pray to. He had been stripped of so many different things; the land was different; the fields were full of men made to be slaves too fearful to even protect themselves against an enemy that oppressed them. They were conditioned to like the oppression, to embrace it, and because of embracing it a better life was promised in the afterlife with this thing they called God

Abram felt defeated. He had no men, no army, no blade. Now here was this pale man trying his best to take the last thing that even mattered to a man simply trying to stay alive.

His pride he replied "may God forgive you."

Peter whispered, "My God don't help no dirty niggrahs."

Abram took a sudden blow from the butt of the rifle, striking Abram's jaw. He felt bone crack under the weight of the hit. All while Mr. Collins urinated on Sarah while staring at Abram like an alpha male dog does his territory, all without a word, totally humiliating Abram, and Sarah as they lay there in shame; powerless in pitiful to the point of feeling below the lowest coward. In that instant they both knew something had to change, one who had never tolerated oppression will never submit to such. You can curtail revolution, but the fire of change itself would always remain in the hearts of those who rather meet their fate.

Scott started to cry running away from the barn, he thought Peter was such a good man. he believed his father was a great businessman, hurt by the loss of his mother. But what he saw was a bloodthirsty rapist, who hated women. Treating a person worse than the stray dogs that roamed free around their plantation. Scott was confused and traumatized, what he observed was not his father, it was something else. Scott had gotten his first live experience of chattel slavery; how could a child understand? Many other children like Scott had to bear these terrible scenes.

The boy slipped back into his house quietly and made his way back to his bed. Scott looked at his hands he couldn't stop shaking. He sat the lamp close by his bed that night, he was terrified that a monster would come into his room. A monster that would do those horrible things he saw being done in that barn, but to him. He would never have imagined a monster like that could look just like his own father.

CHAPTER ONE

Inheritance

Mr. Collins sat proudly at the dinner table with his wife Mr. and Mrs. Collins had been married for 5 years now. They had their first child together with them at the table.

"Big Boy," Mr. Collins said gently to his three-year-old son Scott.

By this time Mr. Collins had established himself. He owned land that was passed down to him by his father and slaves to tend to the fields and labor work around his property. Mr. Collin's stared into his wife's eyes passionately while she held his son, his attention went to his father's gun collection. The couple was only 18 when they were married.

Mr. Collins's father had been a devoted soldier in the Revolutionary War just seven years ago. He'd fought in the decisive confrontation for the land he and his family now lived on. The battle of 1781 at Yorktown Virginia determined the outcome of the Revolutionary War and earned his father the name *'Sudden Death Soldier'*. Mr. Collins mused to himself as he looked at the weapons in his cabinet: five long barrel Kentucky rifles and Flintlock pistols along with his father's sword, an Italian falchion. The blade was still tainted with British blood.

"Thomas Collins Jr," Mrs. Collin's walked in swiftly snapping him from his brief flashback. "I have Bible study tomorrow are you attending?"

His wife was a faithful church-going woman and somewhat of a missionary, going as far as South Boston on the North Carolina line to bring the gospel to whoever had an open ear.

"Oh, sure my lady."

Mr. Collins never really supported his wife on missions but attended church from time to time. Mr. Collins was a prideful man concerned only with the slaves and property since he was a youngin. Mr. Collins remembered his father fighting in that 21-day warfare. He could hear the cannons offshore of Yorktown from French and American forces against the British ships. Stains on the wooden floor with his father's blood dripped for what was their so-called country, America.

Mr. Collins still owned the slaves his father had promised freedom to for fighting alongside him in the battle. Slaves had few options at this point. The naturalization act was in full of effect and the term white came with a more than gracious benefit package.

A sudden memory came to mind, one that had changed him and his wife forever. One cold October night the *Sudden Death Soldier* came back home, but not alive. Fellow Frenchman carried Thomas Collins senior home after British Lord Cornwallis and over 7,000 British troops met a George Washington and led 17,000 troops in Yorktown. It was the battle that won the war for the Americans. Thomas Collins Sr. lost his life.

Mr. Collins's eyes filled with tears as he stared into his father's gun and sword collection. He turned and picked up his son from his mother's lap.

"Scott, your grandfather was a courageous man. He left us a home with plenty of servants which one day will be yours. I promise son, I will show you how to make your family proud like my father made me proud."

Mrs. Collins listen closely; she never truly took to slavery. Being a Christian, she would try to turn her husband away from such evil. Mr. Collins would never listen. He would continue to degrade negroes as his father taught him in Mrs. Collins once invited a slave, DeMarco, to a Christian revival service, a church member informed Mr. Collins of the suspected guest Mr. Collins called all his slaves to the front yard young and old DeMarco looking surprised, Bible in hand. He approached slowly Mr. Collins on Horseback rode full speed towards DeMarco, whip in his right hand. He struck the slave's face so hard that he ripped his eyeball out the socket. Mrs. Collins screamed while the church informant held her back.

"Pick it up," Mr. Collins demanded his slaves. Pointing at the youngest male he said, "Pick it up or I'll hang you upside down from the church rooftop and till your dirty black nigger skin turns red with everyone watching."

The young boy picked it up and handed it to Mr. Collins with the bloody eyeball veins hanging covering his fingertips.

"Now you all know I have my eye on you. Jesus said an eye for an eye tooth for tooth. Amen."

"Amen," All the slaves said in unison and looked on in fear. Mrs. Collins looked in disgust as her husband's evil character came out, evil like a dark shadow, only the shadow had a pale face.

A year passed. Around harvest time, Mrs. Collins became terminally ill with dysentery. Mr. Collins watched his wife deteriorate for months before finally becoming bedridden. Her frame was borderline anorexic. The disease had swept down on the plantation hard, infecting most of the townsfolk. Mrs. Collins got the worst of it, running fevers daily with bloody bowels. The outhouse reeked of endemic fate, her skin rotted off her body with pus-filled blisters, the lonely groans brought tears to her husband's eyes as he lay beside her.

Yorktown's doctor, Franks, diagnosed her but no treatment he prescribed seemed to work.

"Mr. Collins, only eat from your harvest, the livestock is too risky. The disease has proven fatal, Mrs. Collins doesn't have much time."

The news was unbearable to Thomas. On one knee holding his wife's hand while holding his pistol under his chin with the other hand yearning to go with her to the grave. Then he hears a cry from the back room.

"Scott," He couldn't be so selfish as to take his own life when he had an obligation to one that they made together.

News got around to the church community. It became known that now there will be no stopping the cruelty, no second thoughts of aggression in his treatment towards slaves on the Yorktown Plantation.

Mr. Collins had a vendetta, a taste for blood, and his hands would surely draw it. When preparations for a loved one's death are upon you it humbles you, it reminds you of what is inevitable, your corpse will one day nourish the earth.

***

The funeral service for Mrs. Collins spread throughout the town. The small Anglican church Mrs. Collins did missionary work for was very supportive and tolerant of the Natives and Africans. Now the American slaves that had grown close to Mrs. Collins came to attend and pay respect.

The preacher opened with the Lord's prayer while the pine box hung over the hole in the earth. The gravesite was closer to the forest. The tree line led into the wetlands and swamps. You could hear the moans of loved ones and church members from the whimpering of shedding tears for the pure at heart. Even members of other local puritan churches attended to pay homage to this pious woman Hellen Collins.

Mr. Collins sat there trying to be strong with Scott in his lap front row waiting patiently for the preacher to begin. Shall we proceed? The preacher asked while scouring the crowd before looking at Mr. Collins in pity. Mr. Collins nodded, telling him to proceed. Isaiah chapter 57 the LORD said:

The righteous perish,
and no one takes it to heart;
the devout are taken away,
and no one understands
that the righteous are taken away,
to be spared from evil.
Those who walk uprightly
enter into peace;
they find rest as they lie in death

Now Helen was a righteous woman always spreading the gospel of Jesus Christ, aiding the sick. She was always concerned with the hardships of others. The dramatic heckling and sniffling noses grew louder as the preacher continued.

"Uhh mmm," calmly clearing his throat. "She was spared from evil the Looord said because of these righteous attributes. The illusion of a new country comes with old grave sites and bloodshed ah, disease, betrayal, rebellion ah these new lands new people, new customs we have obtained, the colonies we have formed the churches we have built has this new settlement not come with consequences?"

The calamities of this world Helen Collins did not deserve to see, Mr. Collins thought to himself while looking up towards the tree line behind the preacher. A slight breeze sliced through his cloak with a slight chill from the coastline. His senses heightened; the mist of fog floated through the trees along with hanging moss that had a haunting yet serene feel to it. Kind of like the calm before the storm, a dog from the back of the funeral service runs towards the tree line. Mr. Collins's initial thought was the dog would be engulfed by the muddy morass in the dismal swamp. *Tree niggers*. It was like a whisper a faint voice that sounded like his father's. In the Gullah territory, his father would drink firewater and spoke belligerently about when he was with his war buddies.

***

The white man would tread thin back there, barely speaking of the Stono rebellions, the African and native escapees. The invisible war stories of encounters with a Freeland people that fought fiercely.

"Amen."

Mr. Collins snaps back to the grim reality of his beloved's death.

"Let us gather and pray," The preacher formed a circle with all who attended the funeral service. Some Puritans and Yorktown Euro-Americans couldn't even stand to hold hands with Native American and

African people. Even in some cases, the Indians were called niggers too because they simply couldn't tell between the two.

When the funeral ended, Mr. Collins took Scott over to his horse and carriage while being met with condolences from the church. A hand takes a firm grip on his shoulder.

"Thomas," it was Peter, an elderly farmer from town. "I'm sorry, Thomas."

Mr. Collins gives him a humble nod.

"Do you have a moment? I lost my dog during service could you help me fetch em?"

"Towards the swamp?" Mr. Collins replies.

A lady church member offered to watch over Scott, waiting close by and somewhat eavesdropping on their conversation. Peter started walking quickly in that direction, waving for Mr. Collins to follow every step he took towards the swampland. The more he thought about the quiet war stories his father had spoken about, the more intimidating the energy from the forest was as he got closer. Upon entering the forest, they saw tracks and followed deep down into the swampland, further than expected.

Peter called out, "Kody, come here boy! Where are you Kody?"

Noises from the bush had Mr. Collins paranoid gripping tight to his flintlock. Peter's voice echoed through the woodland traveling straight into the bush, Mr. Collins turned slowly to his left and saw Peter's dog, an arrow through the head, castrated testicles in the animal's snout. Mr. Collins immediately whipped out his pistol scanning the premises, there was a shadow over this swamp land. He called Peter to the murder scene. The animal cruelty took him by surprise. He fell on both knees in deep silence. The silence had Mr. Collin's head on a swivel, he looked up the pine trees to what looked like a body towards the tree top. He uses his thumb to pull the hammer back.

"No, two funerals today are enough Thomas!" Peter cries out loud. He stood there glaring at the tree, "There's someone up there, the tree niggers."

***

Peter held the dog's lifeless body in his arms and then in one motion threw his pet over his shoulder, "Let's head back quickly Thomas. Your son is waiting for you."

As they made their way out of the swamp it was complete silence. The men knew this swamp had eyes, the kind that followed you the minute you step into the marshlands. Thomas stayed a couple of paces back pistol drawn looking back frequently in paranoia, he thought this could only be the actions of savages without regard to life, or maybe revenge; a warning to those that crossed over deep into the depths of the swamp. He had just buried his wife, now this random heinous slaughter of an innocent pet dog. All speculation started to sink in, the trip seemed longer traveling out than it did entering and the creeks seem wider while crossing. The crickets seemed more in sync; the sound was overpowering.

Peter had such a serene demeanor about this whole ordeal. Mr. Collins saw the blood oozing out of the dog's mouth over his shoulder onto the back of his trouser pant leg.

"Your dog's name was Kody? Does he usually roam out on his own like this?" Mr. Collins began his interrogation, simply feeling that in this neighborhood Peter was just too calm about his pet being mutilated after a funeral service of a righteous church lady that happened to be his wife.

Peter spoke in a soft tone, looking right into Mr. Collin's eyes, "Mr. Collin's, you don't remember me? when you were a young boy me and your father-"

"Shh," Mr. Collins heard a noise a few yards into the bush, "Who goes there?"

"It's the Pow! The red niggers!" Peter said with an infuriated expression.

At this very moment, Mr. Collins knew that this was the same man his father fought with in the secret war deep in swamps; he remembered the matching fury in his father's voice. He could still smell the scent of rum on Peter's breath when spit came off his lips. They drunk while pouring and getting their wounds stitched, and those eyes... yeah, the eyes never lie, it was as if his soul was on fire.

Taking a deep breath Mr. Collins asks, "Where is your rifle, Peter?"

As they made it out of the forest, Peter told Mr. Collins the Pow were not usually this close to the Yorktown tree line. That's why he didn't think to bring his rifle along with the fact he was intending to pay respects not got to war. He tells him that there must be a reason why they're closer, they are strategic and resourceful. Knowledgeable of terrain, he starts rambling on about near-death experiences with the escapee Africans and the Pow that fought alongside each other. Even sometimes served as missionaries for the red coats. The British promised the pow their land and the niggers their freedom. Yet the Naturalization Act was in full effect and nobody was considered free except the so-called 'White man'. They made it to the cemetery where his wife was buried. The church left a note on Mr. Collins's horse and carriage telling him Scott was with the congregation. Peter was digging the hole a few yards back, he went and watched Peter digging. They said a quick prayer, eyes open watching the forest. It felt like the forest was looking right back at them.

"I've killed many Red-skinned in my day my rifle and blade are my best friends. Then came your father, the *Sudden Death Soldier*. Peter had a humble spirit but was empty at the same time like he was without a soul. The red coats formed some sort of alliance with the tree niggers they attack unorthodox mostly surprisingly or an arrow from treetops. Mostly using the escapee Africans for the guerilla forms of killing. The Africans were the heart of the army, some even went to war with only their hands and feet using some foreign fighting styles never seen by any soldier."

Peter looked at Thomas while pointed at the forest. "Some even dove headfirst into cannons, the fearless beast they are."

Peter's fist clenched with anguish as he talked through his teeth.

"The Powmen are savages, using arson to set fire to our military bases and trenches. I faced off with a tree nigger once while on horseback during a mission to stabilize the York River. Your father and I were anxious to shoot our rifles and volunteered thinking it was going to be red coats we were attacking. General Patrick Henry sent us with 50 armed Africans fighting in exchange to be freemen but soon going into this we learned the niggers ready for battle was a reinforcement for what was waiting at the river."

Peter was envisioning the story in his mind. He could hear the mud under his boots with every step, he could remember the miles of pushing the cannons in position. His breathing became more controlled and he barely blinked.

"The niggers attacked from the left flank on foot, the Powmen Indians came from upriver on horseback avoiding head-on gunfire. Our ranks were easily penetrated. We were separated, then the featherhead charged me. I pushed my bayonet into the horse's chest. The horse reared up and threw the bastard off. I ran towards him with my dagger drawn, I tried stabbing the rib cage but he grabbed my wrist and spun me around like a minuet of some sort, into a chokehold. Then I heard the war cry. It was very distinctive, right into my ear and then my scalp became numb. The blood ran down my eyelids with the sound of my flesh being cracked open like a melon peeling back layers of flesh."

Peter removed his top hat. Mr. Collins saw the open space on his cranium with no hair growth shaved smooth off. For the first time in his life, he felt truly horrified by the sight of an injury. The patch was fire red and grey spots randomly around it told him that infection had set in at some point.

"Dammit, Peter the Pow did this?" Mr. Collins was squinting his eyes.

"Blood'ee bastard did you not listen to the got damn story son?"

Mr. Collins looked down in shame.

"Your father saved me in that fight, firing his rifle hit that savage right between the eyes," Peter was acting out every motion, it was like he could still see the battlefield along the river, he was in his memories of a soldier and he became very tense and aggressive in body language.

"I'm just an old soldier Mr. Collins, but your father was a warrior. He was the safeguard of our small platoon. The story goes, that your father the *Sudden Death Soldier* would lay under a dead redcoat for days using a possum tactic to ambush the British with the blade, waiting for the right time to strike. When a medic or soldier would bend down to treat the wounded, he would silently slice their juggler. Quiet kills for a silent war."

Mr. Collins stood there listening, he turned his head from Peter's curved scalp towards the tree line of the dismal swamp. He felt spooked by the movement of the shadow-like figure in the tree. Kody's castration was stamped into Peter's mind, pointed to his dog's grave. His face red as communion wine.

"This was what those savages do to humiliate you, to mess with your mind and break your will. I will not be broken lad, I will still fight for my land, and kill every one of those savage beasts."

"Amen," Mr. Collins mumbles while walking towards his horse. "Go ahead and finish up Peter, I'm mounting up. Have to get my boi."

CHAPTER TWO

War of the Knives

The War of the Knives (1799)
North Hills, Haiti

French diplomat Hedouville was a master of manipulation, instigating a feud while playing both sides. One was the leader of the Haitian revolution, Toussaint, and his army brigade to the north. The other, Andre Rigaud a mulatto collaborator, and his army to the south who were trying to stop Toussaint's expansion on Hispaniola. The mulattos had a false sense of superiority in economic status in comparison to the black slaves on the island. Hedouville had developed an imaginary line between ex-slave and mulatto who was somehow closer to the French colonist that raped and abandon their mothers to never claim them as their own. The divide between the mulatto collaborators and the ex-slaves was more about pride than about social status. Both sides had already been dehumanized by the Europeans. Ironically the Haitians were fighting for liberty against a traitor who thought he already had it.

The battle wasn't just a battle of brute strength but a psychological one as well, but in war, there is no time to intellectually debate only bloody gore and horrific murder. A seven-hour march with the 'Idol of workers', Moise, the nephew of Toussaint himself. The night before there had been a gathering with the sturdiest soldiers in the infantry around the bonfire, the calling to the god Ogun, the god of war. Most of the Haitian people went back to the African religion of Vodun, using nature as their weaponry. Botany for poison tactics and blow darts from camouflage positioning.

Abram, feeling strengthened by his ancestors marching alongside the coast. The breeze was slight, no match for the beaming sun. This island called Haiti was now home it was beauty at its best, even in the pursuit of vengeance and betrayal by a supposed mulatto of Rigaud's army.

"At ease soldier," Moise said to his 1st infantry soldiers as he walks down the line meeting Abram face to face.

His machete reflected the glare of the light off the waters of the Atlantic, sending a glare that made Abram escape himself for a brief period. Long enough to imagine a woman or creation of pure excellence by God himself. Abram was strong and courageous but like any man, he was lonely for companionship, and the feeling of someday finding a partner in love ironically inspired his vicious motive of attacking with hatred.

The enemy consumed so much of his time with constant awareness to protect his life and freedom. He was angered at the fact he had no time for love from a woman.

"Forward, march!" a loud voice yelled.

Towards the pier fishermen had been gathering their catch for the day. Civilians often felt safe on the island along with merchants and priests who sat near the ocean in peace, or at least as much peace as they could find, with the cannon shots and Naval battles at Sea. Bodies would wash up from Jacmel beach all the way to Petit Grove.

A local farmer approaches Moise while horseback. He calls for halt to his brigade of troops. The farmer informed Moise about some rice he had for his soldiers and intel on how the British traders made deals with the mulattos on the shoreline piers. Moise was accompanied by 50 cavalrymen before disappearing in the nearby bush beyond the beach.

Upon his return he sent some of his cavalrymen, all very firm and serious men, to inform the first infantry of the plan of attack and distribute rations before the battle. Along the shore, Abram noticed merchants gathering as a faint sound of a chant of some sort caught his ear. He turned to his brother-in-arms for an explanation.

"Musa!" Abram said with concern, "What is this call I hear so serene floating in the wind so smoothly into my ear Musa?"

"Look at your shadow Abram," Musa replied.

Abram looks anxiously. Musa was an elder, a veteran soldier that fought on many missions with General Dessalines and survived. He was missing his left pinky, with half his ear blown off. Along with thick keloid scars along his chest and shoulders.

"It's a small time after the peaking of the sun," Abram analyzed the ocean and its position under the sun. "In humble respect Musa, I see that nature speaks to me in many ways, it's midafternoon. Another day to fight and die for freedom against the enemy is my duty as I travel on my journey as a warrior."

Musa looks down on Abram proudly with his seven-foot frame placing his arm around his shoulders, "Yes Abram this is a perfect day to kill but sacrificing your life for freedom is what made you warrior."

Musa was filled with wisdom, strength, and honor. Always finding a way to smile amongst his brothers while turning into a fully raged killer in the face of the opposition. Do you see those men, Abram?"

He looked, "The men in rows facing the eastern part of Haiti?"

Musa tells Abram, "These are the descendants of Abukarri's fleet from the Mali Empire. They lived with the Tiano people on mother Haiti. These are the Muslims."

Abram puts his rifle to his back and starts his walk towards the ocean he washes himself in the Atlantic, then made moves toward the Muslims. With every step, he remembers his roots. His mind drifts into a trance, captivated by the calling of the Ahdan.

"Bondye," he mumbles under his breath.

The revolutionary soldier had embraced the Vodun, the bond with nature, verily his lineage remained in his heart. He was young the memories were vague but the feeling was always memorable. Spiritually drawn, he made it to the ranks and locked his right ankle against his brother's left then began to prostrate in humility.

As Abram prayed with his eyes open, he noticed several calvary men joined in the prayer, side by side ankle by ankle all in peaceful unity worshipping their Lord. This turned into a deja vu moment for Abram as if he was returning to a natural state. The motions were familiar to his body, the recitation from a foreign tongue memorized. While still in a prostrate position. "As-Salaam u Alaikum Wa rahmatul" ah to the right shoulder, then to the left.

"Formation," Moise yelled with ferocity.

"Yes sir!" The men shouted in unison as the ex-slaves got into proper position and continued to march towards their reality.

Moise with a 4000-man army consisted of 2000 cavalrymen armed with bamboo shields and German hunting swords. Some of them even wore gator skin armor around their forearms. 2000 were infantrymen, armed with the 1777 muskets that had flooded Hispaniola along with the Europeans during the Napoleonic wars.

Equipped with French weaponry and trained in guerrilla tactical weapons as the soldiers of the 'Idol of Workers' used in striking techniques. Being that most of the men were farmers, the sneak and power attacks were most effective in up close hand-to-hand combat.

The blade served as your right hand in the striking in Moise's unique fighting style. Sickle blades, initially used for cutting sugarcane had been repurposed into easily accessed weapons and slaves developed a brutal way of utilizing the blades on human flesh.

The up-close and personal style of combat was to Moise's liking, being able to study his uncle and Dessalines' attributes to lead and maneuver. Moise was more than ready to engage. Moise then revamped a Hannibal of Carthage form of attack as many did use Hannibal's great commanding skill and relentless war runs. Shifting towards the south, Moise sent 1500 soldiers into the bush to meet with some Maroon hubs and to flank the enemy.

Moise had already sent out 100 recon soldiers to stake out Riguard's camp ahead of the march that morning. The same brave men returned to Moise and told him how secure the perimeter was. As soon as Moise received the intel he designed his attack. Abram's heart raced while anticipation filled his blood. Moise would bait the Mulattos into preparing for head-on warfare just as their allies the French like to fight.

While he and one hundred cavalrymen would lead a flank attack from the western mountain terrain, giving his army a better chance to avoid heavy rifle and cannon fire, the Haitians geographical knowledge was superb along with science and math for accurate coordinates. Abram made his way out of prayer back into formation, he felt his warrior spirit rise, it was time to kill for the sake of freedom.

Rigaud, with his collaborator army, had some loyal French soldiers on their side, ready to ride with the self-proclaimed higher-class mixed blacks. He tried to position his cannons in the direction of Moise and his cavalrymen, plotting to go for the commanding officer, causing confusion and sending the Haitians into an eventual retreat. With Moise crossing over the Mountainous area just as Hannibal of Carthage crossed the Alps with elephants to conquer the Roman Empire, he would destabilize the cannon fire and have a clear victory.

Back towards the frontline Abram and the 1st Infantry heard the Haitian drum signaling the enemy had been spotted. Musa was in front of the fleet, rifle in hand, spear to his back.

"Ogun is with us, today we fight for our freedom," Musa's hand digs in the earth as he rubs the soil all over his face while running down the frontline looking at each soldier in the eye.

Moise moves into position while Musa ordered the soldiers to take aim. The soldiers were looking down the sights of their rifles.

"Aim for the cannons," Abram heard Musa command.

Everything was in slow motion now. His breathing was steady his heartbeat was rapid he knew one cannon shot could kill dozens of men. The initial gun fire is crucial. Haitian soldiers were eager to get close as possible for their most effective attack.

"Fire!"

Abram already had lifted and fired in one motion at the first cannon he saw. Almost simultaneously shots went off on both sides, two men fell on Abram's right side. He reacted quickly by kneeling and grabbing his comrade's sidearm pistol gracefully placing it in his trousers within seconds he finds Musa had survived the gunfire they reassemble and charge towards the mulatto front line, roaring like black panthers thirsty for collaborator flesh.

Abram locks in on the first mulatto victim as soon as he is in arm's reach, he sidestepped while pulling the flintlock, instinctively cocking the hammer lining the pistol up the mulattos left temple. He pulls the trigger, the gun roars explosively, blowing brain fragments like red sauce skewing from his head over his right shoulder, his life was over.

Immediately Abram flips the gun to utilize the butt, the enemy is steps ahead. Another soldier swings his blade at Abram but to no avail. Abram ducks, then front tumble rolls only to come out of motion continuing full speed ahead through enemy lines. The sound of steel-on-steel clashing made his eyes wide as the night owl. The war moans from bones breaking made him scream to the top of his lungs while holding his machete.

A bullet streaked past his face; it was like he saw and heard it in flashes of light. He saw the rifle fire from his peripheral and turned, only to lock eyes with a teenage mulatto boy. The boy kneels trying to reload his weapon, knowing hand-to-hand combat with Abram is certain death, something warm on Abram's back.

"Blood," Abram thinks out loud, looking behind him seeing a Haitian man holding a hole in his neck gasping for air.

He turns back around. In an instant he grabbed the young boy by the back of his neck pulling him towards him into his blade. He drives the steel into his gut twisting it up inside his sternum, then shoves him away, clear of his blade.

The 1st Infantry is penetrating deep into Rigaud's first lines of attack. A horn sounded some hundred yards back. Moise and his shielded cavalrymen begin to charge the heart of the mulatto's formation, these men with white horses and mostly dreaded locks were expert horsemen, who came ready to slaughter. They rode into battle in a spearhead position. Abram caught sight of his comrade Musa limping back into the protection of the cavalry Abram quickly reacted and acted as a crutch for his brother, placing him back into a commanding position.

"Abram, call the men back into formation," Musa said with blood in his mouth holding his rib cage.

Abram screams for formation raising his machete to the sky, "Back into rows men. It's time to end this, it's time we make our freedom real. Grip your blades, load your rifles and kill the traitors!"

Abram, identifying with Moise's calvary strike followed the blood trail with what was left of the Infantry, with Musa injured he had to think fast. He tore his garb to wrap around Musa's ribcage. He needed to get him to be able to defend himself so they could seal the victory.

"Go Abram be free," Musa said with an evil smile.

Abram lays Musa down on the sand then charges towards the heart with the calvary. Moving swiftly, he finds himself in a bloody circle of chaos, he stutter-steps with his blade drawn with both hands feeling exhausted balancing his grip. A French soldier sneak attacked him from the back in a choke hold position trying to slit his throat.

He blocks it with his arm; a sacrifice to protect his juggler. The sickle ripped through muscle. The gash opened exposing artery and white meat. Abram spun around only to see the same blade headed towards his gut.

He blocks down with both arms. The blade hooked his femur. He hears the bone crack, tried to react but his body collapsed on the sand.

It had a soothing feel on his back as he lied there in paralysis the Frenchman stood over him ready to strike him fatally. Suddenly an arrow from an eastern direction was lodged into the soldier's neck. Moise, in his order of war, had archers behind a tree line stationed like modern-day snipers helping his soldiers in hand-to-hand combat. His perimeter protection was genius.

Musa screams, "On your feet!"

Quickly, Abram's mind reaches for the sound of the voice. Vision blurry, he grabs the bloody blade. He's still breathing, he still must fight! A young archer helps Abram regain his focus and guides him back into the ranks then disappears back into the bush. The enemy lines have been broken. *Victory is near,* he thought to himself as he held his forehead in his palm.

"Left!" An infantry soldier Cezar screams. "Enemy on horseback!"

Abram whispers to himself then he identified with his target, clearing his vision then steadily locks in; with only the knife that ripped his flesh he knows what to do. Abram was limping trying to run towards the horseman he scoops the sand up in his hand within feet of the attacker he thrust the sand into the soldier's face. The mulatto soldier was shocked by the maneuver. He pulls the horse back standing the beast straight up on his hind legs!

Abram then takes advantage in a limp jogging motion using his left arm to grab the mulatto, pulling himself towards the beast and the man then finally he stabs the horse on the buttocks to keep steady as he hoists himself on the saddle. The horse screams and panics kicking frantically, blood bursts like a volcano out of the stab wound. Both men get lounged off the horse it seems like forever before Abram lands on the ground, the only sound was his back striking the hard ground made him realize he was had been thrown.

"Ahhh!" A painful scream comes with the gritting of teeth upon landing on the ground. He had risked his whole body for one kill but this was the way of the Haitian soldier; so resilient and lionhearted amid battle.

The Battle of Knives had been won but not without deep war scars.

"Stop the blood," his comrades replied as they helped him to safety. Abram woke up in the barracks with his brother-in-arms, Cezar, mending his wounds.

"Yah man were hurt badly, you must rest," Cezar spoke with the heavy Jamaican accent.

"I shed blood for Haiti and I'm a villain while the American Revolution is glorified," Abram randomly speaks while grunting through Caesar stitching his wounds. "Have you seen Musa?"

Cezar stutters, "ye-ye yaw maun. He lost his leg to cannon fire. Do not worry he will live," Cezar said with great pride. His accent was thick and Familiar to Abram's ears.

"Liberty looks different to the Americans maun," Cezar answered calmly.

A brief silence was broken by a soldier's concern.

"Did we win? Did we defeat the mulatto Army?" Abram asked with both hands holding his thigh.

Cezar stopped the stitching while looking directly in the eyes and said "Every last one of-of those traitors except Rigaud. He escaped somehow by cowardly retreat."

Abram closes his eyes with a grimaced expression on his face.

"Where you hail from soldier?" Cezar asked, changing the subject quickly as he felt Abrams's blood pressure rising. He knows he must keep Abram calm to slow the bleeding and to secure the brace on his cracked femur bone.

The flashbacks came like a lightning bolt through Abram's consciousness, sending him into a deep trance when Cezar asked this question.

"Abu," Abraham whispers.

The water was filled with fish as Abram looked at his and his father's reflection on the ocean. The tide was high, the food was plentiful, Freetown was home. Abraham's father spoke, walked, and talked in the warrior way. He protected the land of Leone; he told his son, *"Look at the Sun, his is one of the only things that he could depend on to bring life."*

The sun's rays were too powerful to stare into.

Eli was a bounty man, killing and capturing perpetrators was how he fed his family. "Abu, how do you catch the fish?" Abram asks his father.

"The fish are like men. You bait them with the desired temptation, lead them into your trap and you decide to enslave them, kill them or let them go. The mercy of letting them go free fills your soul but the benefit of knowing how to capture them puts you in the position of power."

Abram remembers his father saying, "Never let your power overwhelm your mercy, Abram. The balance of both will bring you closer to God."

Abram was always captivated by his fathers' speeches, giving him insight into how nature and man were so close yet **GOD** was ruler over all. Eli was the descendant of the founder of the Songhai Empire, Sunni Ali. His people had migrated closer to the coast because they were being betrayed by greedy African slavers in the capital city. They exploited their people and traded bodies with Portugal for guns and European currency.

Eli, Abraham's father, never condoned in that. He always remained loyal to his ancestors and their land why would he trade with the Foreigner that had nothing to offer but a false sense of power. Sierra Leone had everything; agriculture, diamonds, mineral wealth, and gold.

They would remain free of Europeans who would deceive them out of the only things that made them truly rich. Their culture, land, and its people. This was exactly what the colonizers, new in the richest land of natural resources they have ever seen, desired. And they manipulated and backstabbed the Africans to get it.

Eli would track these slavers up and down the Ivory Coast, staying loyal to the Mali Empire and protecting his family and people from the plague of the transatlantic slave trade. The civil wars went on way before Abram was even born. The Africans that had collaborated with the European fought against Africans who stood tall with their king and fought to keep the invaders out.

The collaborators, who did all the pandering and shameful deceit among their natives. Eli had wanted them dead.

"I am from Sierra Leone Cezar, but Haiti is my home," Abram said finally, released from his memory.

The many battles they have fought together, all the meals they have split to survive just to make sure the rations would last them the mission. Blank stares in the marches together while sitting around campfires cleaning muskets and drinking rum. Yet they never let none other than Haiti left their lips. Their hearts were in the shape of this island. The objective was to kill for it; to die for it. Being ex-slaves fighting for liberation against so many enemies, there was no time to dwell only to block out any distraction of the mission. The bond was built on the survival not only for themselves also for the land they now call home.

Most of these soldiers had a common connection, and it was betrayal. The trust issues of the ex-slaves ran deep. Being tortured and worked to death, their babies were killed or turned into the property for European profiteers on this soil. It made them vengeful.

The slaves of Haiti wanted equal opportunity, but the equal opportunity to the Haitian warrior was revenge. There was no forgiveness and Abram and Cezar's vendetta made them immortal. It made them obsessively in love with the smell of blood.

Cezar tells Abram to brace himself as he pours rum over the open wound on his leg. Abram grimaces as the acute burning of the alcohol fills his senses, but he bears it silently.

"Abram, we have had spent a lot of days 'ere together in Haiti when I got here to this I... to Haiti,"

Abram looks at Cezar, waiting for him to speak. "I was beating badly Abram I cannot speak like you. I go blank, my mind is not riiiight ting. In Jamaica, the white man was brutal. Abram, he ripped my fa...fa... he was ripped by horses, my ma' was sent to sex farm, sh...shhhee was bred like an animal."

Abram looked on in pain as Cezar struggled to tell him his life in Jamaica.

"I saw her cut oo... open while with child inside while white men laugh and make bet on who dies first. Dis why I ha-haa-te white man."

His words were chilling to Abram. This man had been his comrade, his brother in battle, yet he had never known the personal pain they shared.

Abram looks at his comrade while holding back tears, "We bring dem glory now brother we are san of san blood of blood."

They both sit there staring at each other with tears in their eyes. Tears of despair from two lonely warriors, driven by revenge and suffering. The post-traumatic stress set in on them, Cezar turned to the small fire. He had built beside them he marveled at the orange flame. It sent him into hypnosis he couldn't snap out of.

"When will this end, the memory of agony, violent pale face leaders, broken families with babies being treated like butchered meat? Bein feed worse than dogs and sleeping with the pigs."

Abram spit blood on the earth, "How did you learn how to kill?"

Abram watched Cezar staring into the fire as he spoke, "I was sold here after my family was sold to the sex fa fa-arms. I was sent to this Island white men called Hispanola then I just run. I run far and far then I found the mar-oons deep in the swamps. I meet strong soldier, he teach me about boo- bookman and he sho' me how tah fight."

Abram admired his brother; how he clenched his fist while looking up with his head high with pride as he was illustrating his adventure. *So resilient and courageous,* Abram thought to himself. Abram became tired, the pain was taking a toll.

Cezar asks, "Abram you fight like king maun you run towards death, how about you bruda who taught your sword maun?"

Abram didn't speak but, in his memory, he saw the boat. He saw his mother screaming at the people, the greed in their eyes, the blood in the sand from his father's chest, the arrow was stuck straight up. Most of all he remembered the feeling of helplessness as he and his family were separated and the feeling of the knife to his neck being forced onto that piss and shit-filled boat. That was it, that was the beginning of a warrior's journey.

"My abu he was a soldier, he was free until the European came first to Bunce Island with rum, guns, and Jesus. My abu enemy were the collaborators. He sho' me my blade, he sho' me my fist he taught me survival. My abu was brave. The white man wants to kill me and take dis land, I will die for my freedom."

Abram took a deep breath and laid back, slightly moaning from his leg wound. "My wife woo, wo-ould of made us some plantains in Jamaica. Abram, I miss her so-"

Cezar was interrupted by a scream. "Ambush!"

Before Abram could move, he heard the hammer on the rifle cocking back.

"Get up slave."

***

They were surrounded. The perimeter was overrun by Rochambeau's French fleet, the fleet that controls the man-eaters. The barking got louder and louder. Then he heard the sound of wild dogs being let loose screaming women and children. Some soldiers were tied by the hands and forced on foot back towards the south shore line.

The soldier's prayed for reinforcements from Toussaint, not knowing he was occupied fighting towards the north hills. Cezar pitied Abram, forced to walk miles while barely able to stand. He dragged his leg along, cringing with every step. The French soldiers followed closely with Rochambeau's flesh-eating dogs.

Abrâm knew they were being taken to the French naval ships to be tortured and some killed. Abram could smell the saltwater of the Atlantic, they were close now. He remembered the last word before they were captured, Cezar talking about his wife. A wife was one thing Abram had been yearning for in his heart and he kept it there. A free life, and a family, away from all the fighting; it was a tantalizing dream. But the safest place it could be was there, under the conditions of constant warfare, continuous bloodshed even with man-eating dogs snarling at the blood dripping from his wounds. The thought of love was still there.

Abram was losing a lot of blood, he became dizzy.

"Fre," a faint voice to his right.

"Musa," Abram thought he was seeing things.

There he was on a crutch, half his leg blown off, a rifle on his back. "Don't worry Abram, Ogun is wit you. I called on him to anoint you."

"Arrêtez ici!" The French soldiers began to yell.

Impatiently waiting on the next move, Musa swings his crutch as hard as he could trying to strike a French soldier. He would rather die than live on any longer. He missed, falling to the ground. Their captors just stood there laughing at him.

"Avez- vous faim?" The soldier asked his dog while stroking the animal with his hand. Abram knew the words: *Are you hungry?*

Musa defiantly glared at the soldiers and said, "May my flesh turn to maggots in their bellies."

The dogs were set upon him in the next moment. It wasn't a quick death.

The sound of Abram's comrade being eaten alive made him grind his teeth so hard he swallowed pieces of molar. He kept his head down, trying to hold onto whatever was left of himself. He said nothing and looked only at the ground until they reached the shore.

Everybody was lined up in front of the ships while Rochambeau took his pick, some got headshots, some were lynched or burned alive.

Abram wasn't so lucky. He was taken for interrogation. As he was hauled into a French prison ship, all he felt was numb inside and out. At this point, all he wanted was a glorious death, but he wouldn't have it, not today.

CHAPTER THREE

Fate

"Qu'est-ce que Toussaint's next move slave?" Captain Lubek spit straight into Abram's face, close enough for Abram to taste the rum dripping from his mustache.

Abram inhaled the blood in the room, the walls have been curved by human fingernails from brutal interrogation.

"Tu parles esclave francais? (You speak French slave?)"

"Esklav ki moun? (Slave to who?)," Abram whispers the Creole response but it was too late.

He saw Captain Lubek's blade, it had turned reddish-black from rotten flesh. Captain's face was bloodshot.

"Le seau," Lubek screamed, a French soldier kicks the bucket to him. He grabs it, never taking his eye off Abram for one second. Abram knew he was done talking, it was time.

The blood-encrusted dagger went across Abram's feet each slash getting closer and closer to the bone. First Lubek started towards the toes and then he worked his way closer to the ankle.

"Aaaawwww!" Abram's stomach-turning cries of agony filled the corridors. The seamen that heard the horror eagerly came to watch.

"You will tell me your commander's strategy!" Lubek eyes seemed solid black, there was no soul inside.

Abram looked at the bucket. Inside were dozens of enormous rats. He could hear their jittery squeals. All of them were ecstatic about the scent of Abram's blood.

"Pieds," Captain Lubek said while pointing with the knife at the rat-filled bucket.

Abram was stood up, his hands tied behind his back. The French soldiers and boatswains looked at each other, grinning, knowing that Abram was sure to give up the intel needed to advance and counterattack.

"Mwen pito mouri. (I'd rather die)," Abram growled out while in a pool of blood from his feet. His foot was shoved into the bucket. The rats covered the gashes. A soldier sees him struggling to pull his foot away and grabs his leg, holding it in place. Only then do the smug grins of the onlookers turn into shocked faces.

Struggling to keep balance Abram screams with tears flowing freely from his eyes. His scream came from deep in his soul, so loud, so pained, that they carried throughout the ship, seeming to echo far into the distance.

He had no idea how long it lasted, but finally, his foot was pulled away from the tiny ravenous jaws in the bucket. Abram looked directly into Captain Lubek's eyes. The wind was heavy rocking the ship.

"Liberty or death. You will burn in hell for dah blood you have spilt!" Abram collapsed right there in front of the French seamen and soldiers.

The bucket toppled as he did, spilling the rats who scattered, mouths still bloody with Abram's flesh. Abram lay unconscious while his body convulsed with seizures on the floor.

Rochambeau enters the deck with his beastly man flesh-eating dog strolling beside him. The French soldiers on deck are in a saluting position. He looks down at Abram and his mutilated feet.

"Who is this slave?" He asked, slowly pacing back and forth in front of Abram's body.

"A fighting nègre." Captain Lubek tried to explain but Rochambeau intercedes.

"I have no interest in this slave. My dogs are full of his friend's flesh I need this ship sailing west for I am forced by the treaty of allegiance. The Americans need reinforcements in Florida and I need British pounds."

Rochambeau throws the map at the skipper, "Au revoir. Load the cargo."

The French soldiers drag Abram's body to the bottom deck. The heavy chains clamped onto his ankle and the foul stench of captivity rouses him. The sudden excruciating pain in his feet made him rip what's left of his garment and tie it tight to his feet.

"Abram," A voice from the darkness called to him.

"Who is that?" Abram knew he was losing blood he had to stop the bleeding. He elevates his feet above the cesspool of the cellar and ties the fabric tighter around his wounds. A slight rain starts as the water drips down from the top deck. He uses the rain water to wash what he can of the gashes on his feet. His thigh was still wrapped from Cezar's tending to his battle wounds. The blade went deep but his comrade was able to stop the bleeding.

"Help me!" Abram yelled to no one, with what felt like tears in his eyes but none rolled down his cheek.

The anchor was released, the course was set. Abram continues to stop the bleeding of his wounds he keeps thinking about that voice he heard in the darkness of this bottomless sunken cesspool. It sounded like his father's voice. He was delirious, trying to get his thoughts together, having no idea where the ship was set to sail. He hears the cellar door open without seeing any light.

"Who goes there?"

There was no answer. As Abram tried to crawl closer to the sound in the darkness he gets stopped in his tracks. The clank of metal reminds him that he is chain linked to a body at the bottom of the brig.

Captain Lubek's voice comes out of the darkness," Wake up lads. Bread and slop will become your favorite dish on this trip if you don't die first!"

Abram sees him going down the line, his pale hand holding a lamp. The sound of the slop splattered over each prisoner's area. The captain carelessly threw the cold gruel in a body's vicinity Abram listened as prisoners licked it off the floor.

"Wake up, wake up fre, time to eat. You must eat something," he said to the motionless body beside him.

Abram sees the lamp. Lubek's face slowly comes into view.

"How's your feet lad?"

"Fuck you, coward."

Before another word could come out Abram's mouth. He was struck hard by Captain's elbow knocking him completely out.

"How is this slave even still alive? Go fetch that nincompoop from the deck and throw him down nere' with him. Maybe they can survive their first prison sentence together."

"Aye...aye, sir." Said one of the crewmates who followed behind the captain.

***

Up on the deck, Cezar had been tortured with waterboarding and intense verbal and physical harassment. Cezar spat out salty seawater while a sack covered his head, the seamen continued to pour and pour. Cezar's wrist and ankles are tied down. The coarse rope is cutting into his skin. He was struggling to survive, being constantly plagued by a controlled death sequence. Right before Cezar would drown to his fate, they stopped the flow of water over his face. It was like he could see his soul ascending out of his body then suddenly it disappeared.

Cheated out of a perfect day to die, to the point it wasn't the torture that angered him, it was the fact he couldn't die at the moment he thought verily was his eternal rest.

"Haaalt!" Quartermaster Pierre shouts out at the treacherous seaman standing over Cezar's body with tin pails of seawater. "Take him to the cellar, Captain's orders."

The seamen grab Cezar up under his armpits, his body is limp while his feet are dragging behind him, the bag still covering his face. Cezar tried in vain to shout at the savage seamen but nothing came out of his mouth.

The rage was there but there was no strength left to remind them of how vile and cowardly they were.

Cezar could smell the excrement at the bottom of the ship getting closer and closer. He wanted to pull his arm back to resist but couldn't, all was lost within his warrior spirit. He couldn't fight, at least not yet. The sound of the steel cage bars shutting behind him made his spirit shiver a bit, his eye bulging out of the socket, trying to scour through the pitch-black musk and sewage slush in the brig. With each step, he tried to muster up the strength to call out to Abram, but he just couldn't find the energy.

Another step, his legs folded under him. Cezar's body fell limp.

"Bring me help, Ogun. I suffer long time, make the pain stop." Cezar's prayer was so faint you could hear the chap crackling on his lips as they moved.

The ship rocked sailing west on course to a new destiny for all the men aboard, the journey across the deep abyss while a prisoner of war. Now a prisoner to the sea, the unknown darkness of the water world ahead of them. The bloodshed these warriors have suffered through could fill an ocean. An ocean full of innocent cries of ruthless murder; waves of tears from destitute wives whose children were used as alligator bait and fathers as casualties of war. Two warriors navigating through an ocean of their volatile reality which was pure turmoil, blood from scars re-opened by the whip. This was their ocean.

The ship swayed in a back-and-forth motion on the surface of the ocean. It slowly drew Cezar into a quiet reverie of nothingness. He let the ship's voyage take him on an unknown path to meet his new beginning.

***

Week 40 at sea

There was no sun in sight, only dark clouds roaring with thunderous vibrations that rattled the whole ship. The water from the waves that were smacking the topsail.

Captain Lubek was high up in the crow's nest screaming straight into the storm with an advantageous tone, "Grab the helm lads, hold steady on the mainsail!"

Abram and Cezar are being tossed all over the place by the grips of the storm, slamming them into the walls with every thrust of wind.

"Abram!" Cezar screamed.

Abram responds, "Brother!"

"Are you ok?" Cezar asks.

Things came to this very moment; the strength of nature was a reminder of how fragile man was compared to the supreme power. The irrefutable forces of nature have remained the victor over mankind, since time immemorial, but few get to experience it like this face to face. The cellar doors door is suddenly thrust open.

"All hands, on deck. Now men, move it!" Quartermaster Pierre had the fear of God in his eyes. He was drenched, shivering while his lips were dark blue.

Abram and Cezar looked at each other immediately. They knew the look in a man's eyes, they had seen it too many times before. The sound of keys came across each of their hands and ankles. Both sprinted towards the cellar door up to the deck and the ferocious storm above. Abram reached the deck first and the wind almost swept him clear off the deck. He grabs the hammock net barely regaining his balance.

"Cezar!" Abram reaches to grab his comrade's hand through the heavy rain that hit like darts pricking their skin.

"Yaw Maun I see the rowboat close by the swing guns. We can beat tis we can -" Before Cezar can finish, a wave spills over the deck washing men away rapidly.

Captain Lubek, still up in the crow's nest of the vessel, was limp, his body swaying with the rhythm of the storm. He was holding his arms up to the clouds like he was praising the heavens. He had surrendered himself to nature. Abram held on to a metal handle on the deck while hearing men scream then vanishing into the ocean. The waves were pitch black along with the sky. The only time he could see was with the striking of lightning in the clouds.

The lightning looked like it was striking the ocean, making the quick glimpse look as if things were frozen in time. What matter was time in the strongest part of the storm in the center of the middle passage? It seems as if time was nonexistent. This was never going to end only with death. The only way to endure this disaster was surely death.

"Abram over here," Cezar waving his arm on the side of the rowboat. This was their escape into what seemed to be a glorious death into the depths of the ocean. "Abram, we have to cut the rope, we have to cut the rope now," Cezar had to strain his vocal cords just to cut through nature's rage. Out of his peripheral he sees a man frantically steering the ship wheel; it was Quartermaster Pierre.

"Pierre," Abram screamed. "Let me help you."

Fighting through the blistering rain Abram made his way towards him, both hands gripped to fist with eyes of revenge, the anger made him fight the wind with every inch of his body.

"Grab the wheel lad," Pierre looked defeated and scared of death. Abram could smell it and he also was close enough now to grab the dagger he kept on his hip each time he and Lubek came to the cellar.

Abram quickly replies, "I surely will." Abram snatches the dagger while grabbing Pierre's neck simultaneously, shoving the knife deep inside his liver. "Look at me."

He turns the blade.

"Abraaam!" Cezar's voice sliced through the storm again as Abram pulls the dagger out of Pierre as the storm's lightning flashes in his pupils, he turns back towards Cezar while the body drops behind him. He made his way to the rowboat dagger in hand, "Cezar I have the dagger to cut the rope."

Abram dove in and began frantically slicing the rope. He passed Cezar the knife to do the same.

"I rather die with my brethren in the depths of the ocean with honor, than struggle sailing as a slave on this ship full of cowards!" Abram shouts over the roar of wind and water.

"So be it," Cezar pulled Abram in to embrace him. They saw the wave coming towards them, this was it. "Brace yourself, brother."

***

The ocean's strength carried them out into a new world, an undiscovered abyss that no man has mastered. Abram felt like he relived his whole existence.

"Abram! Abram! That was me calling you in the cellar. I was with you; I love you son."

Abram was in a different setting; he was in connection with his ancestors, now he felt at peace. He saw his father's face.

"That was you abu?" He said to the phantom of Eli.

"Come to the light with me Abram. There's so much peace here, no more killing of men, no more worry, no more rape of women, no weapons, no diseases, no poverty, no violence. Oh son, please come with me."

"But Abu I must fight, dey try to take my land father. Dey killed my friends, some eaten by flesh-hungry dogs, lynched, shot, starved, and tortured. Father my soul cries out for vengeance."

"Remember what I taught you. Fight for the right reasons, your revenge will not bring you glory. Your Freedom, your liberty is your revenge and it is a victory for us all, even those who have crossed over. Now Abram, if you want to keep fighting you mus' wake up."

***

The sun was beaming down on Abram's face, the sky seemed so close to the ocean.

"I thought you were dead maun. You been slee-sleee-sleep for days now." Abram looked shocked. He was afloat in the rowboat with Cezar, alive?

He tried to speak, his throat was parched, his lips like chalk.

"We need water maun or we will surely perish."

Birds. Abram could hear the birds flying above their empty boat but somehow filled with a scorching hot surface. It felt like the wood was on fire burning the heels of Abram's feet.

"Land mus be close brethren the birds are singing," Cezar was bleeding on his side he had suffered from an injury when the boat fell into the ocean during the storm. "I'm weak brother, no foo-food, no drink."

Cezar lays on his back in the boat, eyes to the sky on the opposite end.

"Abram! I saw that what you did Frè, to that maun that time in ba-ba-battle with Dessaline up in th-the hills that day we fight maun."

Abram can only listen to his comrade babble in circles about their war stories.

"You sa-sa-say you was gon blood clot kill that man that murder your friend if you ever seen him again in battle, you remember Ab aa, Abram? Then you saw that French maun you spotted that one maun, den you took that knife you had, you took it and you cut him right up in his neck." Abram started smiling, his skin was so dry it was cracking through the smirk under the sun rays. "You remember Abram ya ya maun you got him you lo-lo-look him right in his eyes while you hold his neck, those was the da-da-days maun."

Abram wanted to say something but all he could do was lay there too weak to even respond. The night fell upon them quickly, Cezar's arm was slightly hung over the edge of the boat, small drops of blood fell into the ocean.

The blood drew sharks, circling and waiting for their fate to become food. The predator's presence began to jump out of the water making the riling the soldier's sense of danger. Cezar slowly pulled his hand back into the boat.

"Blood clot maun," Cezar felt himself being hunted. "Abram! Abram! Where's the dagger?"

He was feeling around Abram's body, blind from the darkness of the night over the open ocean. The clouds had covered the moonlight making it impossible to see anything. He felt the dagger, grabbed it, and quietly leaned back with the knife in hand.

"Jah help us," Cezar whispered.

As he sat back staring at the night dark skies, he thought he saw a small flash of light, lightning was his first thought. But the light came too quickly behind each other, and there was no storm or sound of thunder.

"Land!" Cezar sprung up looking for the light.

There was the hope of survival now, or maybe Cezar was delirious from hunger and thirst and slowly losing blood. Maybe this was some kind of illusion of desperate sorrow while floating in a vast ocean surrounded by sharks and other sea creatures drawn by blood. The diaspora of two men from the land they fought so bravely for. The posterior of Cezar's subconscious was always to fight till death, whether it was with Europeans on the sand or swimming with sharks in the Atlantic.

What was this thing called death to soldiers that positioned themselves in the swamps of Haiti? Having to grapple with alligators just to have the upper hand to attack a French camp. The intrepid mentality of a freedom fighter is the closest to God. These are the ones that would rather be with God himself than suffer as a slave. There are so many soldiers like these forgotten and washed away by egotistical lies and deception. Covered up by crooked men; poltroons willing to go to all cost just to justify oppression.

Cezar and Abram both could be satisfied with an honorable death but their souls wouldn't let them rest. The clock of destiny's hands had turned towards another hemisphere, nautical miles sailed in sorrow, the battlefield is all in the mind when all you did was take orders from a murderous king. But when you are set on a divine path nothing can detour your way, A rain cloud begins to sprinkle life in the boat.

Cezar whispers, "Ogun has heard me."

Haitian mystics made nature their best friend. He gathers water in what's left of his shirt drinking from his hands wringing his shirt over Abram, opening his mouth forcing him to drink.

"Drink Abram."

Abram started coughing in his sleep. Cezar had a close eye on Abram, making sure he didn't suffocate, but it was either this or death from dehydration. In the opposite direction of the lighthouse, Cezar couldn't wait to see the sunrise. He sat staring at the sky. It was cloudy, making it hard for the illumination to seep through each cloud. He had lost count of the hour; the time was unknown. He knew when the seagulls began to speak the sun was close.

Cezar had been up all night, with the moonlight glaring off the pupils of his eyes, his nostrils consumed with the strong scent of saltwater. He lay back again this time satisfied with a torn garment full of rainwater. Closer to the northwest a captain roamed these waters freely. He was a sea merchant, trading and exporting goods from the low country. This captain's name was Joseph Vesey, a slave owner on a Charleston plantation closer to the Gullah Geechee coast of South Carolina.

Sailing out to sea, closer to Bermuda to meet some colonists there for some slave trading and ship repair. The captain's assistant and slave Talamaque, later known as Denmark Vessey. Talamaque was valuable to the captain being he was fluent in several different languages he served as a brilliant interpreter for their voyages. Captain Vesey was frequently moving across the Atlantic to Bermuda, their shipbuilding was superb and Vesey took full advantage of the workers there perfecting the sea vessels for voyages in and out the triangle.

Bermuda had become a hub for pirates and slaves. The first colonist landed ashore and settle before coming into Jamestown. Since then, the convenience of the island served as beneficial for the British parliament. The Bermudan sloop, a ship constructed mostly by slaves, emulated the mysticism of the three points that formed a triangular-shaped area between Bermuda, Puerto Rico, and the Florida Keys. This zone inside of what was called the middle passage, was known to swallow vessels whole never to be seen again.

With an understanding of these points, the Bermuda rigs were built with triangular sails. This configuration proved very effective at sea being the building of the ship was in unison with nature and nautical information obtained by the predated moors and later Mali Empire Abukari III or Mansa Qu, Mansa Musa's uncle, sailed from the ivory coast of Africa in the 14th century to the America's, never to return.

Talamaque was sharp this morning, no stranger to the ocean ahead of him "Captain Vesey the mainsail is catching wind exceptionally well sir."

Talamaque was smiling into the mist of sea looking overboard into the waves. Captain Vesey nodded his head proudly as his sailboat was Bermudian crafted, it cut through the wind and wave so swiftly with agile motions over the aggressive sea currents.

"I need you in rare form today Denmark, we have business to attend to. I need thy to communicate with negro slaves did thy bring your bible?"

Captain Vesey always called Talamaque by the name he felt more suitable which was Denmark.

"Godspeed sire," Denmark replied.

The captain smiles, "Godspeed Denmark."

The sun was starting to light up the sky, breaking through the clouds with streaks of reddish-orange beams intertwined over the horizon. Denmark pulled out his telescope looking out to sea. He took his time moving counterclockwise with his extended eye, he managed to hold still pointing his sights towards what seemed like a small boat.

"Captain aren't we moving southeastern?"

Captain Vesey reaches for his compass, "Same route as usual,"

Demark looks again, "There Captain, look at this," Denmark replies while handing him his telescope.

Captain Vesey immediately commands full sail towards the target kilometers ahead. "Good eye Denmark, maybe these fishermen need some help finding their way back west."

"You think they're fishermen Captain?" Denmark seemed confused asking him.

"Only fishermen would be out at sea this early at dawn this far out to sea mate."

The wind was to their backs, the ocean was carrying them towards what they thought were fishermen. Only if they knew these were warriors for revolution trying to hold on to dear life.

CHAPTER FOUR

Oppression Exceeds the Slaughter

"Almost cotton harvest time Peter. I need to go down to the docks and purchase some negrahs."

Peter looked confused. "You got plenty here. I see you trading off with that mixed breed Indian, kut feathers sticking out his head, black as kolen."

Mr. Collins snaps back, "Gott dammit, Peter. He's a freeman."

Peter holds his suspenders while strolling alongside Mr. Collins to his slave shack, "I need those tree nigger slave traders Peter you know that. They bridge the gap between us and the Powhatan deep in those swamps. They live with the runaways and the rebellious savages."

"I'll kill them both the tree niggers and the Gullah niggers. Yea I shoul' would," Peter tilts his top hat hand on his pistol.

"Just like they did Kody huh?" Mr. Collins stops and waits for Peter's reaction.

"See, that's how I know you'll never be half the soldier your father was."

Peter had the most disgusted look on his face, "My father was a good man, Peter."

"He was the greatest of men son," Peter replied.

Peter grabbed his flask and took a quick swig of brandy, "You taking Sarah with you to the docks?"

Sarah was a slave girl Mr. Collins purchased two years ago. She was of a dark caramel complexion with seductive features that stood out on the plantation. It was like her skin was painted on, barely a blemish, only thick deep distinctive scars on her back from old dirty slave owners whose complex of being infuriated with themselves for being infatuated by her undeniable beauty. It manifested into built-up anger projected onto an enslaved black native woman.

She arose upon hearing two men chat outside the shack.

"What em say, Massa?" Sarah heard her name and said this in a timid voice.

Mr. Collins kicked the door open holding his handkerchief over his mouth from the musty smell inside the slave shack.

"Giit dressed we going down to the docks,"

Mr. Collins enjoyed taking Sarah with him around other slavers, she drew so much attention everywhere she went, it was automatic slave owners wanted to talk some type of business with him, even though he knew he would never sell her. She was the ultimate billboard for a successful business.

"Now you know things got out of control with some negrahs inland towards Richmond area. Some negrah name Gabriel, yea Gabriel Prosser, rallied up some field negrahs and they plotted to kill some good white folks. Some house niggrahs gave up the plan to they masters and they lynched him good."

Peter's demeanor changed, "Yea been some gossip about Gullahs and Seminole negrahs down south too, banning together some fort down there and dem island niggrahs giving the Frenchmen hell out in the ocean. People talking around the plantation's women and children not feeling as safe lately."

Mr. Collins had heard about the ruckus but wasn't concerned he had all his ducks in a row along with plenty of cotton fields, his slaves were broken well. There was no tension on his property nor any fuss about it being anything suspicious around his fields. Mr. Collins had purchased Sarah after his wife passed away. He got her from a native slave owner who lived west heading inland, told him he found Sarah here. Supposedly she was the daughter of a Mattaponi interpreter woman who was killed during the civil wars with another native rebel group in Virginia.

This was a time for indigenous groups. It came down to either you were an ally to the colonizers or an enemy to the colonizer. Ironically, no matter what choice you made the Indian, black, and Seminoles were always the enemy to the colonizers no matter what side they chose.

"Sarah let's go, time to head down east," Mr. Collins said with a stale voice, as Sarah used her saliva to clean her face.

Sarah started thinking about her time at the docks as she quickly hopped in the buggy, never making eye contact with Mr. Collins. The memories traveled with them on the same road she was robbed of her dignity.

"Haaw!" Mr. Collins yelled while snapping the whip on the horse.

Sarah had been to this show before. It was not just any show but a show of naked black bodies side by side in stables by the herds waiting to get shown off on stage. The one thing that stood out most to Sarah on the day she was auctioned off to the same man she was sitting with, were the sounds of pale children running around the stages, laughing, and giggling without a care in the world. While the colored children looked traumatized, tears in their eyes knowing that their future was in somebody else's hands.

The colored children holding on to their mothers, looking around in confusion and fear. They couldn't understand why the pale children could run around free and careless while they could not. Then it was the pale man calling out numbers so fast, to a crowd that cheered and was ecstatic about their purchases. It even seemed like important people were there, like people with some sort of power and influence on the people that attended. The images were embedded in her brain, she would never forget even if she wanted to. The smell of saltwater made her extremely nervous. Her hair rose on her arms and neck, her body language reeked of fear.

"A lil thirsty massa," Sarah said bashfully to Mr. Collins. He handed her the flask. Staring forward, she wanted to jump out of that buggy, she began to do one of the only things that made her feel well. Sarah sung:

"Someday life's journey will be o'er
And I shall reach that distant shore
I'll sing while entering Heaven's door
Jesus led me all the waaaaay
Jesus led me all the way
Led me step by step each daaay

I will tell the saints and angels

As I lay my burden down

Jesus led me all the way"

Mr. Collins kept his eyes on the road as Sarah's voice blew chills up his spine. The smooth melody of her strong voice touched his soul in a different way. He started thinking about his wife, how much he missed her. He glanced over at Sarah only to find her eyes closed on a trance of brief harmony. A path so familiar to Mr. Collins he began to question was this his legacy? These docks?

Was Jesus guiding him on the divine path of human trafficking, for agricultural free labor? To take women from their kids, and torture black men to the point of humiliation, of lynching and castration? Was sweet Jesus leading the way on his journey to do God's work? Or was it that he was more like that jew who plotted to kill his God? Mr. Collins could never choose righteousness over his lifestyle.

"Give me that water." Mr. Collins said while snatching it out of Sarah's hand cutting off her voice.

"I sorry masa," Sarah began humming this same melody to prevent her heart from dying.

The smell of saltwater was thick in the air now they were getting close. Sarah could feel every bump in the road feeling every bit of anxiety she was praying mentally but passionately. Even T\though Sarah was beautiful she never truly knew it she was just another negro slave girl and that's how she felt.

"Why God, why? What do I need to do for your help please answer me?" Sarah whispered in her prayers right beside the devil himself.

"Sarah, I don't care to hear no crying today, you gon help me fetch some new negrahs for my cotton and it's bout time you start pushing some babies out yah hear?" Mr. Collins had a serious tone.

Suddenly he spots something in the road. He commands his horse to slow down. They both fixated their eyes on what was on the path in front of them, a beautiful big hawk in the middle of the path feasting on what looked like a black snake. Sarah stared in amazement. The hawk spread its wings over its prey with great pride while picking at his flesh. The hawk's talons were closed tight with one quick gust of wingspan to thrust itself off the ground.

"Haw," Mr. Collins yells. "Why did this damn horse stop like that?"

Mr. Collins was livid as he wanted to trample the damn bird in the middle of the trail, how dare that interfere with his journey to the docks, who did nature think it was to delay his business? Sarah felt a sense of entitlement and she also started to feel satisfied. Her mind became clearer, her tears were gone. The birds were chirping loudly with the horse's hooves was in unison with her heartbeat. The sun now energized her soul lite beads of sweat cooled her caramel skin.

Nature speaks truth to those who can interpret the message, Sarah knew her prayer was answered. Now all she needed to do was understand the sign God had sent her. Her spirit was encouraged a feeling of guidance secured her anxiety.

"Faith," Sarah whispers.

Her moments of fear turned into courage ready for what was to come. The sight of sand and a festival-like scenery appeared just over the hill there. Sarah knew the vibe; Mr. Collins wore a gluttonous grin as the crowd grew bigger, surrounding a high stage. The flutes and Mandolins were high pitched, black top hats were close to the maiden dresses as they spun in the wind to the sound of the instrumentation. The children were overjoyed by the atmosphere, protected by American soldiers that stayed busy loading whiskey and gunpowder onto ships alongshore.

"Well, hello, Mr. Collins."

Mr. Collins immediately recognized the voice, "Captain Vesey how are you today?" Mr. Collins kept in good relations with different sea captains. "You dealing in stock today?"

Captain Vesey started to reply no, then he remembered the two black men floating at sea barely holding on to dear life.

"This may be your lucky day Collin's." The captain was a merchant and wouldn't pass up a sale on anything worth selling that he got from the ocean. "I may have something of interest for you."

Mr. Collin's eyes widened at the gesture, "I'll follow you then I suppose."

Mr. Collins directed his horse forward as he began to stroll behind Captain Vesey on foot. Closer to the beachfront he saw Minister Quinn. Mr. Collins had to stop to speak to the man who did his wife's eulogy. The Minister seemed excited, waving while lightly jogging towards Mr. Collins's horse and buggy. He held his bible tightly beside his right hip.

"God bless, God, bless you all now. How is everyone on this beautiful day the Lord hath made?"

Mr. Collins took off his hat in respect to the minister, Captain Vesey was looking back with a facial expression overwhelmed with impatience.

"Minister, what a pleasure today to see you down here on this wonderful day. What brings you here today on the beautiful York River?"

"Oh yes, by the blessings of Jesus Christ I have come to preach the gospel to these savage souls. They must be civilized somehow, son."

A long awkward pause led Minster Quinn into scripture

"Ephesians 6:5 Slaves, obey your masters with…"

Captain Vesey quickly cut him off, "Now, now Minister, no disrespect but we are running late we must handle some slave business. Now, please pray for us to make these savages whole and sold because we got to go now,"

"Okay, yes, yes my apologies beloved. Any shillings for the church today?"

A short chuckle from the unnerved Sarah.

Both Captain Vesey and Collins reached in their trousers, "How about her?"

"Mr. Collins, she looks an exceptional negro here," Minister Quinn pointed at Sarah with his bible in hand.

"She not for sale preacher," Mr. Collins whole energy changed, Minister Quinn slowly started to rub his beard as if he was in deep thought.

"My condolences once again to your wife Mr. Collins,"

Minister Quinn looks at Captain Vesey before turning to walk away from shore.

"Jesus fuckin Christ that man is a bloody toad," Captain Vesey starts to speed walk towards his boat leaving Mr. Collins and Sarah behind.

"I'll be back mate," The captain yells back to them as he fights his way through screaming children, over the loud music. Sarah is curious and takes advantage of Mr. Collins entertaining small talk with locals, she jumps off the buggy and follows Captain Vesey closer to his boat. She spots a man, a black man dressed nicely. From afar he was directing what seemed to be white sailors to load up cargo onto the ship.

Sarah had to get a closer look she thought. A black man on a white man's boat giving orders? This couldn't be real. Maybe she was seeing things. As she crept in for a closer look Talamaque started to walk off the loading dock to have seat under the shade of the tree line. He reached into his pocket and grabbed his small hunting knife and an apple he had in a small pouch over his shoulder.

He was peeling off slices slowly as he saw Captain Vesey walking urgently towards the ship kicking up sand with every step. A noise from the brush interrupted what would have been a short break in the sand.

"WHO goes there?" Talamaque shouts aggressively while pointing his knife like a compass at the woods.

Sarah stops in her tracks.

"Is Somebody there?" he asked in a more calming manner.

Sarah's curiosity may have gotten her in trouble. Sarah response. "Yes, I'm coming out sire."

Talamaque's eyes were locked on the direction of the voice he heard, "Come on out. No need to hide madam."

Sarah came towards him she noticed something different about this black man. He didn't look, act or sound like a slave. He was tall well dressed. She was shocked by his demeanor amongst the white folk, but the closer she got the more his of his vigor she felt. It made her feel unafraid and appreciative of his existence.

"Oh, you startled me a bit madam. I was just sitting here enjoying the breeze off the ocean here."

Sarah looked around cautiously.

"You act as if you never seen a Freeman before," Telemaque laughed out loud. "Come, come sit down here with me my lady, I come in peace today, I am tired from all the hours at sea and I have done some minor carpentry work for Captain now I must get my thoughts together before we leave from here."

Sarah tucked her dress under her bosom and sits beside him in the sand.

"What is your name sir?" Sarah said looking directly into his eyes.

"Oh, how rude of me," he said as he reaches out his hand. "My name is Telemaque but most call me Denmark, and yours?"

"I'm Sarah."

"Sarah, what brings you here today?" He said with a curious smile.

"I ran down here from Masa' Mr. Collins to see where the captain was going. Do you have a masa Denmark?"

Denmark looked at her with purity and love in his heart for he knew this woman was certainly a slave here in this land.

"No madam, I do not have a master. I have freedom to go as I please and someday you will to my dear," his voice became firmer and more serious as began to move his hands as he spoke. "Sarah, do you know who you are, where you come from, or who are your ancestors?"

He was now looking towards the ocean now, enjoying the tranquility of the waves.

"I don't Denmark."

Denmark bends down now and grabs the sand then releases it into the wind. "My ancestors came to this America many years before the white man, and some white men love us but most hate us. They were from the Mali Empire. His name, Abukarri the Mansa Qu, he was king. His fascination with the sea took over him and he sailed here with many fleets of ships never to return home to Africa."

"Africa yes I hear songs about this place from the field niggas," Sarah became excited.

Denmark corrected her, "No niggas, but negus."

Sarah was confused.

"Then even before them the Olmecs, they were no slaves, they brought the temples and pyramids and medicine, science, they were gods on earth," Denmark knew he was losing her. "Look dere' Sarah."

He pointed out towards the ocean. "There is still hope across these waves. Our brothers and sisters are fighting for freedom against a tyrant and his name is Napoleon. He leads the French, he is an oppressor along with the British, and Spanish. European greed is not just in this land Sarah. It's happening right over the ocean, over the great river, the ex-slaves have fought bravely in the face of evil intent. They have overpowered the forces of the French; they have outsmarted a fierce military of not one but three countries trying to put them under the sword of slavery. They have fought to the death,"

Sarah sat listening to his amazing speech. "There is a great leader and statesman on the front line with the soldiers fighting for liberty right now as we speak and his name is-"

Suddenly a loud voice calls out, "Denmark! Denmark!" He turns quickly southward towards the shipping docks,

"We need your help sire."

He spots Captain Vesey and some seamen waving their arms frantically trying to get his attention.

"I must go madam, but remember who you are, never forget, soon you to will be free. You will be free."

Denmark looked at her with such passion. Sarah pissed herself from the chills that ran up her spine. Her knees weak she never heard a black man speak like this. The vibrations of his voice were one with the tide. His palms were sweaty and his eyes had tears inside them, tears of slight disparity rooted in genuine lust to the point Sarah could feel every part of his concern for liberation. His energy traveled through her, but what was this liberty he spoke of?

Sarah did not know exactly but she felt it in her soul and she knew that this man would stop at no lengths so that one day she would know. Sarah was left in sorrow as his back was to her, his cloak floated in the breeze as he ran slowly towards the seamen. His hat flew off onto the beach, Sarah locked in on it and she ran full speed to grab it with no intention to give it back but to keep it. She wanted to always have a piece of this man, this mysterious sailor who was free.

As she got closer and closer to the hat, she felt freer, and the freer she felt, the more in tune with who she was. Whoever that person was inside of her, she knew now she was destined to find it. Sarah grabbed the hat right before the tide took it. she stood and stared into the ocean looking for something greater than herself to speak to her. Then she realized that the voice she had been yearning for had spoken through somebody and that somebody happened to be "Denmark" Telemaque Vessey.

Meanwhile, Mr. Collins was in the mix of the crowd talking and waiting on the prized human livestock to be presented. As he waited, he began to think about his wife and how much he missed her; he still mourned her, he saw some familiar faces from the church she attended. Even though she was anti-slavery some members of her congregation were very active in the buying and selling of slaves. Mr. Collins by no means claimed to be a religious man or indulged in Christian fairytales and righteous talk.

He knew deep in his heart he was wicked; the lifestyle of oppressing was normalized; his son would inherit land and property built on the backs of people that were dehumanized and suffered in front of him. A life of suffering translated into sacrifice by bible scriptures and false rhetoric from pastors like Minister Quinn.

The children there brought more concern for Scott. Mr. Collins ironically didn't like bringing Scott to the docks. He felt the kids never really paid attention to what was going on, they just ran around clueless not understanding this was going to be their lifeline to propel them to power for generations to come. The wailing of his wife haunted his mind. That was when he realized this had been the first time he had been to the docks since her death, knowing she supported him and benefited from the family business yet she never felt a part of it. There had always been a disconnection between them that they never truly discussed through years of marriage.

Mr. Collins saw Captain Vesey making his way up from the distance. He was relieved at the fact he could bypass the gibberish of the onstage slave auctioning and be able to get quick service and get back to his plantation. Sarah remained cautious following the small entourage back towards the white folk waiting on the auction to begin.

"Mr. Collins, I have this fine negro man here, he is in good shape he has survived solely off bread and water. Very strong-willed savage he is," Captain Vessey's salesman skills were on full display as his scheme played out. After having to haul this poor soul all the way up the dunes he had to make the sale.

Captain quickly set his price, "Thirty pounds would suffice for this body Mr. Collins and we both could be on our way,"

Mr. Collins quickly examined the negro before him. He noticed he had no lashes, no branding on him, or any signs of being enslaved other than his current condition. He was weak and hunched over his skin was extremely dry. He had scars but not like slavery scars. They were more distinct wounds from what looked like a blade and bullet. His hands were huge and rough.

Abram's physique was chiseled with definition but lacked the muscle to match. He was barely holding on to life. Mr. Collins could see he was strong and a survivor.

"Sold," Mr. Collins threw him the bag and called for Sarah to help load his new slave up onto the buggy. "Thank you, Captain, until we meet again."

"Oh, we shall not mate. I'm keeping my place down into the Gullah I have no more business here too far north. Good day mate."

***

Abram was awake, to no avail because he felt like a zombie his body was struggling to listen to what his mind told it to do.

"What is your name boi before I give you one myself," Mr. Collins asked this while holding his head up by his chin and jaw bone.

Abram pushed past the fact his mouth was like cardboard, his saliva was like sand. "Abra-Abram."

Mr. Collins caught the faint reply, "Ok Abra-Abram." He mocked at his weakness. "Welcome, you are now the property of the Sendview Plantation. This here is Sarah and I am Mr. Collins. Allow me to tell you the rules that you must obey by law or receive lashings. Rule number one, you will never leave the plantation without permission. Rule number two, you will never sell anything on the Sendview plantation. Rule number three, you will only be permitted to marry by my permission. Rule number four, you will labor a minimum of 12 to 18 hours a day during planting and harvest time. Rule number five, field niggers eat what they grow. Rule number six; you will attend the negro church on Sunday and will observe the sabbath as I see fit of course."

Mr. Collins looked as if he was done then he added, "And if any of these rules are broken or if at any time any negro tried to escape off my land that pathetic creature will be subjected to the Virginia Lynch Law."

Sarah felt sick to her stomach, she couldn't tell if Abram heard a word he had said, but she could tell that Mr. Collins sure did enjoy hearing himself talk about those inhumane rules. It was time to head back, Mr. Collins helped Sarah up into the buggy, she slid over making room for one more body.

"Nah Sarah, no need for that," Mr. Collins chained Abram's hands and latched him onto the back of the hatch forcing him to walk behind them while they traveled inside the buggy.

Abram looked so weak. Sarah was concerned if he could make the long journey ahead being dragged behind the carriage like that. There were no options, only submission, being forced to watch this man suffer in his desperate attempt to stay alive. Abram let out an evil grin, he was hurt but he had been more damaged before. He was malnourished but he had been more famished, he was parched but he been more dehydrated, he was traumatized but he was a frontline soldier he laughed in the face of death while sometimes even chasing it, to no avail only to lead him here in this mysterious land across the ocean.

He knew he had a chance to grow strong to make it back to fight again with his leader. But where was Cezar? He began to think about the last time he heard his voice. How the ocean was calm, how Cezar had somehow found water even while he was delirious from pain and the heat of the sun. As he kept his feet in front of him as Mr. Collins rode the horse, he tried to feel nature's energy, to see if he could feel a sign that his comrade was alive.

He knew Nature was the only thing that remained in order. He could trust it, he could translate the vibrations at times, he just needed to focus. To focus like when the cavalry soldiers would allow him to sit with them around the bonfire deep in the swamps with the gators to sharpen their blades and pray to Ogun to guide them in war. Abram looked down at the soil of this odd land and seen something familiar, something that gave him confidence in trusting in the signs of nature. He saw the fire ants, reminding him of the importance of the order of nature and how no man is above this order. All the ants working together as a team putting in work making everyone stronger all for one purpose that is beneficial to their whole existence, uplifting their queen and protecting their colony.

Remaining in unison at all cost even if it meant death. One must ask himself who or what is the source of power in your life. In the time of war one can learn from nature. This is what Abram knew because he had been there for all his life, and now he knew the war he fought was bigger than Haiti. The leaders of oppression was trying to conquer the whole fucking world the fight isn't over, Abram was thankful to be able to fight again another day in another land against a similar enemy this is why he smiled His history of violence could never be suppressed only prolonged.

The disadvantage was he lacked an army, yet he knew nature was the greatest ally he could have. He had to reevaluate the terrain the forest was different. The weather was not as humid, to him anyway, the sky wasn't as bright blue. There were no palm trees, and he saw more white men than anybody else close to these docks. Cezar could have easily done some recon if he knew where they had taken him, he was very observant and crafty he was a survivor Abram knew he needed Cezar so they could formulate a plan and establish some sort of map of where they were and how far the ocean had taken them from Haiti. Abram's body may be vanquished.

"That sure was a nice trip, Mr. Collins," Sarah was looking back at Abram to make sure his legs kept moving.

She didn't know anything about this man that was getting pulled by a chain by the horse and carriage but her encounter with Denmark opened her mind to the chances of being free, the journey began with feeling free and the rest follows. Abram made her curious she knew he had come off that same boat Denmark sailed on. She knew there was something about that Captain wanting to get rid of him so quickly and fairly cheap. Sarah had enough experience to know when a negro was sold for cheap. She saw when Mr. Collins examined him and there were no lashes, only war scars. This man had come from somewhere different.

"Eyes in front Sarah no need to keep lookin backwards less you wantin to join him back yonder," Mr. Collins had a jealous tone.

Sarah turned her head and sat in silence, today was a day of transformation at heart for her. As they got closer to the plantation, she became more resistant to the idea of being just a simple slave girl, trying to please her master. Her sadness became self-consciousness; who was she? What was the purpose of life without freedom? How could she obtain it? All these new feelings with no one to share them with and she dare not mention it out loud. She wanted to write it down but how? She was far from literate and to express it meant torture or even death.

"Whooa," Mr. Collins sounded to the horse as he saw another carriage coming towards them on the trail.

As they got closer to the carriage, he saw it was a native man. He knew natives frequently purchased slaves for their land as well specifically some of the Mattaponi people. A tall well-built bronze figure riding on a stallion of a beast sped up on the trail at a pace that didn't appear to be inviting.

"Seke," Mr. Collins stood his ground waiting to have some sort of greeting.

Mr. Collins slowed his horse to a trot so he could assess the situation. Seke was a businessman that had the rights to acres of land belonging to the Mattaponi indigenous. It was land they grew tobacco on for generations however when the Europeans came the uprising of tribal feuds over who would submit to the devious colonialist ways of white Jesus, sneaky smiles, fire water and what started as trading crops to I want to take over your land rape your women then you work for me for free wasn't an option for some of the indigenous.

So, when the white men were killing natives, the natives were also killing the natives who wanted to side with the European powers to oppress their people. Colonialism ultimately won this battle leaving some displaced Native Americans still living off the land, and they were free after almost being victims of genocide. The low-life Native-American slave masters would take on the same characteristics of their white slave masters.

Seke gave Mr. Collins a cold stare. "What you got there?" Seke took pride in emulated the white man, his English was better than most Virginian locals.

"Ah nothing much just leaving the dock," Mr. Collins also thought Seke was up to something. He was quiet mostly until it came to business, he was a money-hungry man.

"That Captain sold me a nigger. We shall see how he works out on my tobacco field," Seke pointed to the back of the carriage. As soon as he did a head lifted slightly above the edge.

Abram saw the movement

"Cezar," he yelled. His reaction was automatic, how did he find the strength to yell?

Seke grabbed his rifle. "Mr. Collins these slaves here know each other?"

"Oh, what does it matter got dammit? Now gone be on your way now," He snaps back at Seke, hand on his pistol.

Sarah looks back at Abram with her finger over her mouth signaling to be quiet.

"Don't say another word," Sarah aggressively whispers to Abram.

"They shall be no trouble on my plantation," Mr. Collins sees Seke slowly put the Kentucky rifle strap over his shoulder.
"Good day Mr. Collins. Haw!" Seke gave his horse a strong whip. Mr. Collins nods his head while uncocking the hammer on his sidearm.

He pauses for a second, then jumps down from the buggy speed walking towards Abram. Mr. Collins whips out his pistol while snatching Abram by his wooly afro and placing the gun precisely under his chin.

"If you eva' speak out of turn like that again, boom!" Mr. Collins fires the gun right beside Abram's eardrum, "Next one will be in your head."

Sarah thought he was dead. She looked up at the sky as the birds scattered startled by the gun sound. She was shaking. She knew at the price he got him for he was expendable. Abram's eyes rolled into the back of his head, he fainted fast then Mr. Collins began kicking him hard in the stomach then the face and head. He was attacking Abram's helpless body violently.

"Stop Mr. Collins Please!" Sarah sounded like she was having a panic attack.

"You come help him then you lil' wench, hold him up the whole way home then, since you can't help but to open your mouth. Help him all the miles home," Mr. Collins was out of breath yelling at Sarah after that display of rage.

Sarah ran to Abram serving as a crutch. She could feel his pain his sweat-drenched her dress. When he lifted his eyes, she fell into them diving into a pool of agony she was drowning in his afflictions. His sweat made her feel the history of torture. He was tense from anguish, distinct sounds kept going from his jaw when she realized that was him grinding his teeth from the pain. She had to come up for air before she too became a victim of his pain through her empathy. The miles seemed like months, it was such a long gruesome walk it was like God put the sun right in the middle of the sky skipping the shade of the trees and beaming directly onto their backs. Sarah felt the trail getting steeper and steeper.

"All's mos dere na," Sarah whispered ever so softly.

They were up over the hill now and Mr. Collins could see Peter from a distance. He was in the fields on horseback, rifle over his shoulder, and surrounded by the Sendview plantation slaves.

"Peter come on over here I got me a new one, come on, come on here Peter," Mr. Collins was smiling as he jumped off the buggy.

Peter had become somewhat of an overseer on Mr. Collins's property. Not to mention he would babysit Scott when Mr. Collins had to leave for business. He fell into the role naturally, even had some of his people that he'd recruited himself. The extra hands were a godsend, especially around harvest season.

"Simon come on here. Mr. Collins got some new negrahs to tend to these fields now."

Sarah hated Simon. He was the definition of a low-life negro. He could barely look you in eye, he had been brainwashed beyond fear, he was whatever the white man was. If the white man was upset, he was upset, if the white man was jolly, he was jolly if the white man was sick somehow he had come down with the same symptoms.

He was the first one at church helping minister Quinn set up and adlibbing every verse all in the middle of the sanctuary catching the holy ghost, he was that nigga'.

"Simon coming," Simon barely knew how to speak the English language. All he did was repeat what he heard and follow instructions.

Peter claimed he got him from a sex farm where he was used as a breeding tool to make more pups, as they say. Rumor is they called him a 'motherfucker' when he first appeared around these parts. "Look here, I want you to make sure these here slaves follow the rules and fall in place out here. Now I don't need no trouble on my fields. Simon is gon keep watch over yall, and don't you even think about asking Lydia to help you out with anything. She stays in the house at all times you hear?"

Mr. Collins had a sense of urgency, being it was about that time to make some money. Sarah nodding, she wasn't concerned with Lydia. Even though that was Simon's wife, she knew she was miserable, being forced to marry a man like that. Simon took her hand in marriage as a gift from Mr. Collins himself for selling his unworthy soul. He bred him with her like a dog, putting tags on all the pups she pushed out. That old savage Simon didn't have to raise one.

Sarah could never find comfort in a house negro woman that was disgusted with her existence.

"Simon, grab the god damn chain lad," Peter was sweating like he had drunk a fifth of whiskey.

"Grab the god damn god damn," Simon sounded damn near remedial.

They tried acting like he was normal but they knew that man wasn't right in his mind. Mr. Collins threw him the key to unlock Abram from the buggy post.

"Show him the shack," Mr. Collins turned his horse gracefully towards his house. Abram's eyes were gazing over the huge amount of tilled land in front of him. He saw corn, spinach, tobacco, and wheat all growing in abundance. He saw who he thought would be soldiers, black men, and women working in the fields.

He was confused, he saw hardly any black people by the shore and now he finds them at least fifty or more singing as if they're happy to be in a wretched place. He had never seen so many white people this comfortable and confident that nothing would happen to them for oppressing black people in his entire life.

Abram let out a deep breath of depressive sadness. He almost immediately fainted. The pain he had suffered from gunshot wounds, seeing close friends eaten alive by wild dogs, even left out to die at sea. But the sight of people that could be soldiers or martyrs for their children's freedom accepting this type of treatment almost brought him to his knees.

Click.

Right behind his head was a familiar sound. He looked back; Simon nodded his head north.

"Brother I shall-" before he could even finish the sentence Simon gun butted him striking him to the ground standing over him.

"Me not your brother," Simon's had distinctive twitching in his cheek, he was more beast than human.

Abram was able to identify because of the inbreeding practiced by the mulattoes. Being ever so loyal to the enemy they subjected themselves even to brainwashing. The mind control tactics of the French were needed to have some sort of diabolic hold beyond a man's word or handshake. To them, you were no man. You were an undesirable; less than an animal.

Abram knew this man was weak. A blow like that from a real soldier would have knocked him out cleanly. He stood slowly, leading with his knee first resting both elbows on it. He held his ribcage; it was sore from that tantrum Mr. Collins threw. His ears were still ringing but it hardly compared to the gunfire he was used to.

He caught his balance then he rose, staring at Simon's gun and thinking if his body had half the strength of his eyes, he would take that gun from him and kill him with the blink of an eye.

Instead, he just continued walking towards the slave shack.

CHAPTER FIVE

Justified Revenge (Virginia Winter 1800)

"While most American newspaper would highlight the action as a Indian fight, it was actually an engagement largely fought by black militia or parties of blacks whom the patriots think are Indians because they wear the same clothing and go painted"

Cezar's teeth chattered as the snowfall came down on his tent. Seke was not letting anybody in the cabin today. Cezar had never seen snow before; he had heard stories of the high altitudes of the mountainous regions having this thing called snow yet he had never experienced it. He wraps his deer hide over him tightly moving towards the entrance of his place of rest hoping to strengthen his fire for survival.

"Cezar, come to the front yard, nigger," Seke had mimicked the Europeans so well his whole plantation thought of him as one.

Cezar was happy to hear his voice travel through the blizzard wind. As he made his way swiftly towards it, it appeared to be three more

Mattaponi men with copper skin all with rifles standing watching his every step.

"Seke," Cezar was taken by the mist of his breath in the icy atmosphere. It felt like he was on another planet the air was different the feeling of the frost biting his flesh was different from any pain he had ever felt. Mighty cold out here. Winter storm coming in hard. Most my slaves on the inside tonight,"

Seke rubbed his hands together in the cold. Cezar patiently waited for the invite to come in as well to the nice wood fire and hot tea.

"I even got my hogs in the back house can't let them freeze to death. hope I can keep you around to keep the hog pins clean for them," Seke smiled as snowflakes lay on his mustache.

He had humiliated Cezar to the point of being a swine herder but Cezar was a master at controlling his rage. He focused on observing the land and watching the movements of the oppressors. Cezar just nodded in agreement, feeling his entire body getting goosebumps from the wind chill.

"I have a proposal for you Cezar. I only have room for one more body in this cabin and my long-time slave boy Sparrowhawk wants it as well. I thought I let ya'll work out the problem yourselves," Seke throws a dagger a few feet in front of Cezar.

Sparrowhawk was a tank of a man with wide shoulders and large hands and feet. He stared at Cezar as he walked down the porch stairs closer to Cezar and closer to the blade.

"Whomever comes out alive comes to the cabin."

All the native men let out a cruel chuckle while holding rifles. Seke pointed his pistol in both of the men's direction demanding action. They dashed at once through the thick snow. Cezar controlled his breathing as he ran not taking his eye off his opposition. Sparrowhawk's eyes were down, trying to find exactly where the blade had landed so he could strike first. Everything was in slow motion for Cezar, his instinct of soldier's survival kicked in as he got closer and closer to the weapon. A soldier was always prepared for battle even when his enemy thinks he is not aware. A good soldier is always aware.

His senses were keen, he was constantly training and preparing for the worst and the unexpected scenarios. This was why he held on to the stone blade he got from Konah the Vodun woman that Seke kept close to the cabin. He kept it in his thick matted dreadlocks. So thick the sharp stone blade he would use to clean fish from the nearby York River fit perfectly into his healthy rooted hair.

All Cezar had to do was lineup Sparrowhawk's jugular vein, "Ogun I call upon you in this strike!"

Cezar lunged at his chest like a wild wolverine, small stone blade in his left hand. The dark stone was camouflaged so well when he whipped it out of his scalp it looked like a small piece of his wooly dreadlock. Sparrowhawk eyes grew big when he saw Cezar baited him into thinking he needed Seke's blade laying lonely in the snow. Sparrowhawk defended himself by putting his hands up in front of his face the stone edge sliced through his index and middle finger.

"Aaaahh!" A noise of pain shot by Seke and his comrades' ears while they looked puzzled seeing the dagger was still laying in the snow.

Cezar fell on top of his target, violently punching and elbowing his temple. After the strikes he quickly grabbed Sparrowhawk's hand while ripping the stone edge blade out from the hand. Blood splattered his face while Sparrowhawk's hand was still twitching.

"Finish it," Sparrowhawk whispered while spitting up blood on Cezar.

Cezar gripped the blade high above his head breathing heavily as a horse that had been riding through miles of valley. He could feel the snow again he could see the blood seeping into the frost like a red slush pile. Cezar began to look into this man's eyes, then he remembered the battle with the mulattoes, how they collaborated with the enemy, how they submitted to their indoctrinated schemes of hierarchy. This man was simply trying to survive as he was in the blistering winter on new land full of cowardly oppressors.

"No," Cezar told him cringing at his own words, "I will not kill this man. Seke you may have us both hung or whipped but I refuse to kill this man, he is no enemy of mine. I rather lay froze in this ice land than spill the blood of this man."

Seke and his comrades looked with smirks on their faces, "Very well, boys take these savages to the outhouse with Konah, forty lashings. Immah pick ah nigga out first thing, soon as the snowstorm has settled."

With rifles pointed at him, Cezar helped Sparrowhawk to his feet. He rose and looked at Cezar in a way he will never forget. A look as if to say, *I was prepared for death but why?* They could hear the chains on Seke's men's shoulders. Rifles were pointed at the back of both of their necks making their way towards the outhouse in the back of the cabin. The old outhouse smelled of piss and shit but Cezar knew he could lite a fire in it to survive the night's storm.

Cezar had a plan. He knew he had to build relationships with the natives to learn the land on how to move, hunt, and recruit a small army. He needed to find the best possible escape route and most of all reunite with Abram.

They were thrown onto the freezing cold floor. Cezar struggled to get a fire started, his hands felt like fleshy ice.

"You stol' that stone knife from the Vodun woman. That witch woman, ain't you?" Sparrowhawk spoke boldly as he pulled out a small piece of match paper and a small piece of a wax candle, cringing from the pain. The gash between his fingers was split open but not bleeding, just meat hanging.

"Here soldier, you are soldier?" He seemed unsure in his assumption to Cezar.

Cezar didn't care, he only wanted to get some warmth so they could survive this thing they call snow he hadn't seen before. He lit the candle and looked around for anything to start a small fire. A small opening near the roof served as an exit for smoke. As they lay, Sparrowhawk had a calmness about him that made Cezar was glad he spared his life, even more, he could tell this man was brave and he didn't fear death.

"I neva returned it afta' eating crawfish from the river. I barely got that damn fish to bait. Why do they call you a Sparrowhawk? There are things I needs to know about quickly. We can defeat these men they are surely weak and cowardly excuses for men they are."

Sparrowhawk signals for him to stop talking, "Your voice is strong, it carries into the wind of the storm into the ears of the Seke people. The wind is my partner in the hunt, I know how it moves. I follow that way I can hear when it speaks to my heart all the way from the ocean from the mountain mist into the forest."

Cezar saw how he motioned his uninjured hand with the sounds of the blizzard winds as if it could have carried him right out of the roof with the smoke from the fire. He seemed so in sync with nature, the way he spoke of it in a delicate tone, like it was sacred.

"My soul is Sparrowhawk," Cezar nodded in humility letting him know I understand now. "Sparrowhawk knows this land I will show you our way I know you hate the white man I can feel it you have to be like Sparrowhawk to kill white man you have to follow my way to live long in this land."

Cezar took a deep breath of the cold air. The fire had grown stronger all their strength was gone as their eyes fell from exhaustion.

***

They awoke to the crowing of the rooster at the slightest crack of dawn. Through the icy aftermath, Cezar's locks were covered in frost. He looked over at Sparrowhawk. He was in a fetal position trying to keep warm, knowing the fire would go out while they slept. The wooden door flung open almost rattling off the handle. It was Seke, pistol in his left, bullwhip to the right.

"So yall savages ready fo' lashins?" Seke motioned them to their feet.

The sun was out, the slaves had been running around chasing chickens and salvaging whatever was left after the snowstorm. It had frozen over during the night. Seke's tobacco and corn were ruined. Cezar could smell the hog slop as soon as he stepped out. Sparrowhawk was slow to make it to the entrance as they both squinted from the morning sun hitting their eyes, the worker unchained them. Sparrowhawk keep looking back at the Konah's small shack a few yards from the outhouse. He knew they would need her after this beating.

"Cezar you get the rope and whip from behind the hog house you know where to look," Seke brandished the pistol in his right hand as he stood on the melting ice. "Hurry towards that pole Sparrow and prepare for lashings. You lost dat fight, now you was spared but I won't be so merciful next time I'll blow your head off clean boi."

Sparrowhawk looked into the sky. He was taken by the gleaming sun off the ice. He did not fear death nor did he become troubled by lashings. As he removed his ragged shirt, the old scars were revealed from previous beatings from Seke. He never understood how this could come from his people. He understood now for years that one's people would enslave you, humiliate you, as if they see can't that you are the same.

The fact was, they don't want to see themselves, they hate who they are. The values of the Euro-American traditions were far more worthy and the power behind the whip had more longevity to a self-hating coward. "Hurry up now boi come on wit da whip," Cezar tried to hand it to Seke, but he refused. "No, you will lash him not me, thou shalt not kill right?"

Seke had an evil smirk. He calmly raised the flintlock barrel to his head. "You will rip the flesh off his back," Seke screamed in his ear. Cezar could only think of grabbing that pistol and go out in epic fail of trying to subdue a bullet with anger. He proceeded to whip Sparrowhawk, with every strike he vowed to kill Seke. He was trying to break Cezar's soul and for the first time, he felt his manhood was taken from him.

***

Cezar felt like he had lost himself. Sparrowhawk was unconscious, flesh was torn from all parts of his body. Nobody dared to help or even look at the body straddled around the pole. Cezar looked at the blood dripping off the whip mixed with thick chunks of skin and muscle. He began to try to untie Sparrowhawk's arms from around the pole. He stops for a second and looked back. There was Konah, the mystic doctor that

Seke keeps around without worry, nobody seemed to know much about this lady.

She was standing in front of the sun rays. Cezar couldn't get a good description of her facial features, she was a silhouette of being, her energy was melodic, staring in peace at the same time with purpose and strong presence. Something glistening off her neck while leaning on what was a staff or large stick for walking. Her head was covered by a familiar turban worn by witches, at least it seemed as such. Their powers and spells proved to be supreme by those who have encountered their remedies.

Konah moved towards the two men, it was as if she was floating towards them without steps. Konah gripped the crystal ball on her chest that was tied like a necklace by old vine and tree moss. As she did this, she took two fingers across the back of Sparrowhawk and tasted the blood.

"Vini, Come," Konah said while smiling, almost laughing.

Cezar looked at her as if she'd gone mad, then took Sparrowhawk over his shoulder following behind this mysterious woman. Cezar was almost brought to tears as he carried him, the same man he had spared he was forced to beat him nearly to his fate.

"Awww blood clot," Soon as Konah open the door it reeked a horrible smell. Konah spun around quickly looking Cezar directly into his eyes. "Shhh, you will surely awakening them."

Cezar now had an up-close and personal view of this Vodun woman. She was fierce, full of unknown forces that made the hair on the back of his neck stand straight up.

"Lay him, lay him," she said pointing at the deer hyde laying on the straw bed.

Konah had chickens throughout the shack, with hanging dead carcasses, metal pots and ruby stones on top of crystals along with old sand scripted writings. He could now see her, Konah's eyes were wide and slanted upward towards her temples. The thickness of her eyebrows brought out the grey hairs showing her age. Konah's nostrils perfectly fitted her face although her unique beauty was mystical. Cezar's attention was with the snakes, the snakes she kept inside an open box hissing at every move they made.

Konah looked down at Sparrowhawk very thoroughly she took in all the damage then she looked at Cezar with a most disgusted look of disappointment. While never taking her eyes off Cezar she instinctively grabs one of the chickens by its neck, spinning and snaps the bird's throat with one thrust. Cezar impressed by her expertise almost missed the chicken's body still running around the shack. She looks away smiling and laughing chasing after the headless chicken's body.

"This wench is blood clot crazy," Cezar whispers to himself trying to close his jaw shut but it was too much. "The gott dam pot over there, friend get dat pot get it."

Cezar stutters in his movements as he moves towards the direction she is pointing. Before he could even turn around to hand over the pot, Konah was stoking the fire. The fire was a blue flame. Cezar had heard about the blue flame of the ancient Vodun mystics; he had yet to see this up close.

"Here you are," while passing the pot over to her he spilled some of the fluid onto his hand, the smell was potent as cat urine and it immediately it evaporated upon touching his skin. Then Konah went into the box of snakes with no fear or hesitation. While the liquid boiled the smell was almost unbearable to inhale. She uplifted a human skull and dry bones holding them to the ceiling mumbling what sounded like jibberish. Konah dropped the bones in the pot along with the chicken head. From the body she plucked feathers she did this very delicately examining each one.

The blood of the chicken went into the potion, Cezar began feeling drowsy, extreme fatigue took over him. Sparrowhawk was grunting loudly turning on his side, it made the flesh from his upper back hang off like red layers shedding onto the hay bed. The fumes from the pot were strong, it seemed like the walls were moving, the snakes seemed to be moving in the same motion as the steam from the kettle pot. The crystal on Konah's neck was glowing or was it the fumes that made Cezar think it was?

"Drink the bones," Konah said, handing Cezar the cup.

Cezar had been caught up in this oracle's transcendental ways of witchcraft. He easily took the cup to drink, her way of hypnosis made him believe he needed it.

"Aaaawwh," Konah snatched Sparrowhawk's head back to drink the bones.

As Cezar sat down with his back against the wall, he started to think deeply. All he had survived to get to this strange land, with people with copper skin like him that had been here for centuries only to become victims of slavery sold out by their kind. He was exhausted, overwhelmed by struggles unimaginable to an ordinary human. Why him? Why so much killing and violence? Cezar took a deep breath while holding back tears of depression of an old soldier looking for something to reflect on besides murderous intentions.

He would be fooling himself if he didn't want to kill Seke, at this moment he vowed that he would, he just needed a moment to accept his circumstances as they are and how it will be until he is deceased. This world he was born in doesn't like him, it hunts him constantly trying to enslave him, to conquer not only his body but also his spirit, his culture.

Cezar has had moments like these before, then he had to remind himself; *the evil in me is a result of the evil that surrounds me.* They must have dozed off his unconsciousness made him oblivious to the hot plate and water beside him as he woke up.

"You must eat Cezar," Konah's voice had a hiss to it, very raspy in tone.

Cezar ate the biscuits and honey savagely, the potion of bones he had drunk earlier seemed to have put a hole in his gut. He was so hungry.

"What was this you gave to us Konah. My mind is full yet my stomach feels like it's been wiped blood clot clean?" Cezar had his hand on his belly. Konah just looked at him with a smirk.

She then reached into the box of snakes without fear and pulled out what looked to be a scroll, Cezar looked in amazement.

"How did you get-"

Konah puts her finger over her mouth, "Shh."

Cezar knew this was an important secret, this witch doctor was trying to reveal the truth to him but why? For what?

"I knows you would come here Cezar; I saw you in my dreams this man." Konah looks him up and down "This warrior."

"Look woman you're spooking me blood clot out."

"Ahhhh," Sparrowhawk lets out a painful grunt.

"Is he okay Konah? Will he make it?"

"Yes, he will make it. The question is, will you make it Cezar? Will you make it to the people?"

Cezar was confused.

"This is the way to the Powhatan chief. He is a strong dark-skinned war chief. The chief's eyes shine like a beacon of light he speaks to the animals in the forest. His horse moves with grace, he has an army of archers and his rifle never leaves his back. He took many lives from white men he hunts his enemy. Some say he even eats their hearts with his featherhead soldiers he is the true chief of this land you see HERE."

As she spoke, she simultaneously pointed to the pictures on the map in front of Cezar. Cezar grabbed the scroll gently looking at the detail Konah had drawn the mountains, the lakes, and nearby rivers. The different native territories. She had the American military bases along with the different plantations closes to them. For a recon soldier like Cezar, this was vital information and now he could plan his next move.

"Konah, do you know the pale maun with ginger hair tall man with green eyes that buys slaves down by the docks towards the river?"

Cezar sat anxiously waiting for the answer because it ultimately would determine the first part of the mission of finding Abram.

Konah looked at her map, "Here."
Cezar immediately identified the location east of the dismal swamp right across the river. He looked at Sparrowhawk, as he turned his head back to Konah she was wrapping his hand around her crystal ball rubbing him with a cold cloth across his forehead.

"This stone has energy of my ancesta' from the early rebellions, forgottin' people that stood up for themselves during a time of treachery. Tonight, I will need to recharge the stone if dere is full moon. Sparrowhawk is very weak he will need all the energy out of my stone. But you Cezar, you have to leave before sunset. Seke will be lookin' for you soon you must take this scroll and use it to attack."

Konah looks at Sparrowhawk's back, "He is already healin. Those bones are special. A warrior's skeleton I dug it up from a old slave gravesite. I cast a spell over it calling to the ancestors fo' power over these wicked people that have captured my people and took everything from dem, the

Gullahs determined to be free and we paid for it in blood. One of the leaders of the Stono times was my great uncle his name was Jemmy."

Cezar looked at Konah, "Who exactly is tis' blood clot maun you speak of and why dis huh? Why you have us drink his remains."

Konah continues to explain the significance, "Fo' his spirit, Jemmy hated the pale man." Konah's eyes grew big filled with pain and a glossy layer hinted at the flowing of tears. "He killed da man that kept him ah slave. He chop his head and put it high on ah stick for every person in the colony to see. He wah from the Ashanti, known for bravery. I watch you since you came here. You stole my stone knife yah eyes full of rebellion. You have no fear of deaf this remind me of what freedom looks like, I am' Geechee people but my heart is with the Powhatan natives they took me in showed me the way of the tribe that hunts from the trees. Do you write Cezar?"

"No, but my bruda' Abram ca-can read and write. This is why I must find my bruda' he is a brave soldier."

Konah grabs his hand, "You will find what you are lookin fo. Now go before Seke comes here. He is a clever man, he brought me here for my magic. He thinks I keep his land safe from the rival natives but no, I summon dem' across the swamp. I know dey hear my cries, I know how to come to them in their dreams. I float past their dream catchers and they know who I am. I am the one, I am Konah of the Gullah people accepted by the Powhatan tribe after the British war."

Cezar takes another look at Sparrowhawk, then he walks out the shack into the cold air back towards Seke's main cabin. He folded the scroll into his boot. Cezar was at ease with the certainty of escape. He went into Seke's cabin secretly looking for the armory and pantry for rations.

"You hauling wood today Cezar les you wants to end up like your friend Sparrowhawk."

Cezar wanted to rip his Adam's apple out and feed it to him but he knew he had the upper hand with the map Konah gave him. All he has to do was wait for Sparrowhawk to get well then, he would make his move.

"Yes sur," Cezar smiled ear to ear.

"Boys, take him to the wood field," As Seke spoke the men went into the third door in the house returning with rifles to escort him.

Cezar counted every step every turn and calculated the time it took for them to return with the muskets loaded ready to fire he knew this was where the armory was. His soldier senses were high as he made his way towards the woodpile. Cezar chopped and pulled the timber while observing the land he knew they were south of the York River he thought about the encounter with Konah, her majestic ways, and the story about Jemmy.

Cezar knew he couldn't be a slave, blending in as a slave was so easy to do just look down and act weaker than someone that you knew you were much mightier than. The breeze was cold and Cezar's hands began to ache with the pain of frostbite. His agony led him to a campfire with some old slaves singing the white man's church songs. Cezar picked his axe up looking for the next tree to chop.

"Raaas clooot!"

That's when saw the men hanging from the same tree, he was looking to chop. Had to have been fresh he could tell by the swaying of the bodies. Cezar begins rapidly chopping the tree down. Back in Haiti Cezar had seen lynching's in the most gruesome way as Dessalines and Rochambeau would use the most sinister acts against each other just to prove a point of bloody revenge on different occasions. Rochambeau had hung a whole village of women and kids. He burned them alive, but not before cutting off their heads. Leaving them for the men to find when they returned home.

The calamities of the two men made Cezar realize the grim truth about the evil that men do. Pride and vengeance cocooned a man into a diabolic soul that manifests nothing but total destruction. Cezar felt every swing getting closer and closer to timber. Other slaves passed him while he hacked at the oak wood, they dare not stop to warn Cezar of an overseer coming. They were spineless cowards scared to even cut a tree that wasn't authorized by their master.

Cezar didn't care at this point he was going to get these men down and give them a proper burial. He was going to do it just as he had done back on Haitian soil. He successfully got both bodies down, then quickly traveled back towards the wooded area where he was working to grab a shovel to start digging the hole for the bodies right along the trail. He did not hesitate, he moved as if he was following orders back in his brigade, removing the dead after the battle was over. He paused for a second to look at the disfiguration of the men. The sight was repulsive, the faces had swollen like a pumpkin with the neck twisted and stretched out unnaturally. These men couldn't have been over 20 years old at most.

Then Cezar saw something he had witnessed before. The men's mouths were full of their manhood. Cezar gagged at the glimpse of emasculation. It caught him by surprise, making him realize these oppressors would constantly find new ways to humiliate, control, and dehumanize him. The deeper the hole became the more tears flowed out of Cezar he couldn't help but feel the agony of these two men on this day of free labor for a self-hating Indian man, combined with the guilt of what he did to Sparrowhawk. Even with a gun pointed at his head, he knew he should have died with honor before allowing a coward to use him for his dirty works.

Why had he come from one wicked land to another land full of scoundrels? Devious, devilish men who bathe in their envy and insecurity towards any brown-skinned being. Cezar could see his breath in the cold air turning to mist just before rising above his outgrowing mustache.

The map from Konah began to slip out the raggedy boot. He reached down to reposition it deeper into the heel when he heard the voices of the overseer's yelling, "Halt, halt nigga boi what are you doing?"

Two of Seke's plantation hands along with a Patriot soldier accompanied them. The sound of metal cocking back got his attention, "Now everyone, calm down. Now, this buck must have lost his cotton pickin mind, diggin' a hole without permission on another man's property. Dead or alive this doesn't concern you, boi?"

The soldier spits in the hole with total disrespect for the dead. Cezar stuck the shovel in the earth then climbed out the hole, "Yessur."

He then spat a lugee into the soldier's face with no remorse. His body language screamed; *I'll die right now.* The American soldier lowers his weapon and uses his other hand to wipe Cezar's mucus-filled saliva off his face, he tucks his flintlock pistol and draws his blade placing it directly on Cezar's juggler vein.

"Go ahead and do it you blood-" before Cezar ended his statement, he had a mouth full of fist laying on the ground.

"String 'em up, boys. We gon watch this nigger hang from a tree just like these two poor wretched nigger souls he tried to bury."

The American soldier had a calmness to him, he had probably killed so many men it was just a job now. This was nothing new, just another low-life nigger to leave hanging for everybody in the wood yard to see.

They tied the rope so tight around Cezar's neck his eyeballs poked out of the socket turning his lips blue. The cold breeze made his hands sting every time he tried to grab the noose around his throat for relief maybe a small amount of air could make it into his lungs.

Cezar stopped trying to relieve himself of the rope. His body lost strength, his bowels released piss and shit that ran down his legs as they threw the rope over the oak tree branch. The two men pulled Cezar's body up over that thick tree branch manually with no second thought they kept pulling until his feet dangled at least 6 feet off the ground.

"Keep pullin' booys. Keep that nigger steady don't break his neck I wanna see him suffocate," as the soldier gave orders, he would randomly lend a hand to stop Cezar's body from swinging. "Hoool steady now," he said with a savage smile.

Everything was black for Cezar at this point. He was content with his fate, he'd rather die than be a slave.

"Enough," A scream from some yards away came from the mist of the woodland, "What is this madness I witness? This is my property; being hung by whose authority might I ask?"

It was Seke coming to collect his firewood and supplies.

"This nigger here was burying two nigger bodies without permission from the owners and he was quite rude to American authority so I decided to have him lynched here by my orders."

"Your orders," Seke replies.

"Yes sir, now you look like a copper skin nigger yourself so you could join him if need be. Sir, move along."

Seke becomes livid. He couldn't handle being associated with no nigger. "By God, I will have you executed by law soldier. This is my land granted to my family by President John Adams for my forefather's participation in arms with the United States army in the Battle of Timbers. This here land was given to us in honor of my bloodline fighting for this soil long before you even picked up a rifle!" Spit flew from Seke's mouth as he spoke with displeasing pride, "Must I provide my paperwork or-"

"No, no, sir please forgive my trespasses on this matter, sir," Seke mentioning General 'Mad Anthony' made the soldiers boots shake.

"Drop em' now," Seke demanded the cowardly laborers.

Cezar looked dead during this whole hanging encounter he was deprived of air to breathe hanging helplessly from an oak tree almost breaking his neck. When Cezar awoke, he was in Seke's cabin butterball naked in front of the fireplace.

"Heelpp," he yells at the top of his lungs, thinking he was still hanging from that oak tree on his last limb of life. His first thought was hell when he saw the fire beside him. Cezar laid back down he was discombobulated, and he kept thinking to himself he rather had died and gone to what people describe as hell than be in this one.

"The map," Cezar looked around for his clothes, that's when Seke walked in from the hallway.

"Where did you get this map?" Seke walked closer to the fireplace with it in his hand.

"I made that map for my escape, but before I escape, I will kill you and I will take your guns. Then I will kill the rest of your men that remain on your land and free all the slaves here."

Seke almost fell over laughing at Cezar's crazy talk.

"At last, I will rescue my comrade Abram from across the river and we will do the same thing there. We are 1st infantry soldiers of Haiti we have fought with the great Dessalines and Moise my blood had spilt on lands far from here. I have even more blood on my hands and yours will soon be on my knife."

Cezar felt on his neck from the attempted hanging hours before the abrasions were deep the blood was dry.

Then Seke drew his flintlock placing it by his side, "You know Cezar, I saved your fucking life son, and now you say you're going to kill me? I persuaded the American soldier to spare your life while you hung by your weak ass coon nigger neck. If it wasn't for my forefathers fighting for this land and being an ally to General Anthony Wayne of the United States army you would be a dead nigger."

Seke held his head up with pride, pistol in hand, "See that is the difference between me and you maun. My forefathers from Haiti bookman to Makandel would never collaborate with the colonizer. They would much rather die in their glory before they work to enslave their people. They would find new ways to kill the enemy. Your family was full of weakling rats, puny sacks of wine that deserve to drink my peoples piss as they beg for it to quench their thirst ashamed of their distasteful selves at the gates of hell."

Seke sat there with his head down in deep thought still clutching his hammer.

"You will pay for those words Cezar," Seke's replied in a hateful tone.

"I will gladly pay in blood."

There was a knock at the door, interrupting the conversation. As soon as Seke looked at the door, Cezar made his move, rushing Seke and catapulting the pistol shot into the ceiling. Cezar pins him by the neck in succession with Seke's knife that was on his hip going into his right cheek. Seke had never seen a man move that fast and that was the last thing he saw. Cezar's locks got covered in blood as it squirted out fiercely from the blade being lodged in his cheekbone.

"I tol' you I was going to kill you and now I will go on killing the ones like you and spilling the blood of the blood clot wicked along my way maun. You're a blood clot coward."

Cezar dragged Seke's body into the backroom, towards the armory. He knew the gunshot would alarm the overseers. They would surely come and he would be ready.

He grabbed a musket and one flintlock, also a sword. He was ready, then he remembered out loud, "The map."

He crept back into the front room as knocking suddenly sounds from the door, growing louder when no one responded. Cezar found the map, slightly damaged by the flame. He quickly took Seke's clothes off and put them on. He tightened the belt, putting the map inside the coat pocket. The knocks turned into efforts of men trying to ram the cabin door open. Cezar walked back into the armory room. He stuffed two flintlock pistols inside his belt. The muzzle loading rifle the British Bess was in reach, on his back with the strap over the shoulder as he tied the knife around the muzzleloader for the bayonet.

He could hear the overseers in the house now finally he took the long saber off the table placing the muzzleloader down it. He would end this with the sword he thought then he quietly waited. He heard the men when they stopped at the trail of blood, Cezar stood by the door and listened. He estimated three men by the steps and voices, he got low by the door anticipating gunfire.

Boom!

Gunpowder filled the air as the men shot through the door. As soon as the men had forced the door open Cezar struck violently. He charged the first man screaming with the sword in front going straight into the victim's chest. He fell with the sword still in him. Cezar pulled out the knife from the belt he got off Seke's body and thrust it into the man's shoulder as he tried to fire his pistol. Then he tried to draw his pistol, to finish the man off when another man fired a shot that clipped his hip.

"Aaaahhhh!" Cezar screamed out.

He quickly fell back into the armory room. He knew he had to kill these men before he could escape the plantation. He got up, holding his hip, and picked up the muzzleloader that he assembled the bayonet on. He could see the man checking on his partner with the knife in his shoulder, even with the bullet in his hip he couldn't let the soldier reload his weapon. Cezar fired the second flintlock pistol towards the men; one on the ground the other kneeled in assistance.

"Fuck, the nigger shot me!" The mixed-breed overseer yelled holding his right arm.

Cezar threw the pistol down, hobbling toward both men. Cezar's blood was all over the handle of the rifle as he took his hand off his hip to hold the rifle properly for a bayonet attack on both men.

"My name will bring fear to the hearts of men in this land!"

The knife cut easily through the men's flesh as they begged for their lives. Cezar didn't even clean the blade. He was bleeding badly, he couldn't manage to carry any more ammo or guns. He grabbed the sword out of the corpse's chest, kept two blades and he threw the muzzleloader down it was too heavy to bear. Cezar raided the house for food and water. He moved quickly as the bleeding from the gunshot in his hip was leaking profusely. He made his way outside the night was quiet with the overseers dead, funny how all the killing brought peace to the work farm. Cezar needed to get back to Sparrowhawk quickly and make his way across the York River to Abram.

"The horses."

Cezar knew this was his only chance to get there quickly. He went to the barn and tried mounting Seke's horse as he tried to jump on the back of the beast. Cezar fell in pain from the gunshot his breathing was heavy his eyes watery. He pulled himself up trying his best to ignore the pain,

"Ras clot maun," he mutters to himself through his efforts, finally mounting the horse, "Whoaa!"

Cezar slowly guides the stallion towards Konah's shack behind the main cabin. For a short walk turned into what seemed like an hour's journey. As Cezar lifts his head, he sees a shadow of a person "Cezar quickly she motioned towards herself." Cezar was starting to feel tired he was losing a lot of blood. Konah helped him off the horse.

"You're hurt Cezar?"

Cezar nodded with his hand close by his groin. Konah helped him in the shack.

"Where blood clot Sparrow?" Cezar immediately asked as Konah laid him on the straw bed.

"He be with us in spirit."

Konah looked surprised. "You kilt dem all Cezar?"

"Aah, raass clooot!" Cezar yelled out as Konah pressed on the wound.

"Issa clean wound," Konah grabbed her bottle of rum and pour it on the quarter-size hole, the pain made his eyes water.

"Naah lays back, lays back. I have tah stop the bleedin' quickly Cezar."

Konah heated the blow poker until the tip was bright orange.

"Bite it." It was a thick wood block she placed inside Cezar's mouth for the excruciating pain ahead. "Hol on Cezar I have tah do this if you wanna live."

The procedure made Cezar pass out. The slaves came knocking at Konah's shack door yelling and screaming in terror. They had found the men dead in the cabin and heard Cezar screaming bloody murder from her shack. They wanted to know what was going on. Konah stepped out into the night with her candle lamp, her presence was felt soon as the people saw her eyes through the light, she held the lamp by the handle close to her face so the slaves could see her concern and feel every word she was about to say.

"I sees sum of yahs weepin' ova'what you saw in Seke's cabin. Ain't no mo' Seke I see some man angry in the crowd here grieving over the same man that filled you back up with stripes so thick yah can see dem through yahs ragged shirts,, I see women in this crowd whose babies were sold inland for shillings to that dead man's expense and still you niggas weep?"

Konah pointed at this one specific man. "And yah are from the Mattaponi tribe dat fought against these tyrants. Yah saw your ancestors eaten by coyotes; your land was stolen only to become a slave to yah own lineage that went with the white man in his dirty tradin of men for fake coins that mean nothin yet you weep over such man?"

"A man that sold his soul, sold his people out to be like the monsters that laid claim to a sacred land that wasn't even his in the first place. I is a Geechee woman me ancestors laid claim to this land long befo' any pale creature my people came 'ere with Mansa Qu from Mali and the moors over the great river and traded with the copper skin people the great chiefs and native nations of this place the white man calls Amerikka the Seminole people are all of us together against the oppressor yah seemed to have forgotten, this life is not normal. I will not accept tis' you are not supposed to be slave don't allow dem to make you feel like an animal rememba who you are rememba your tribe rememba the empiyah. Rememba the great spirit dat protects us, our people showed them how to hunt and farm these lands. Our people ate from this land, we are the land and the land is us so go ahead and cry over cowards. I is free I will die for my free and I will kill for it."

The slaves just stood there in confusion, needing direction. Even with their bondage lifted they asked each other where will we go? What will we do? How will we survive without our masters? All these random frantic outbursts Konah was hearing made her realize their bodies were free to go anywhere, the oppressors were defeated but mentally they were still slaves.

CHAPTER SIX

The Marshlands

Pleasure over pressure, is what Abram thought as Lydia's hand moved down his abdomen lower and lower into his crotch.

"I love you," Lydia passionately whispered to him, sending chills up his neck. Abram took a deep breath, finally, there was no pressure he was in blissful peace. The tight grip of love had held him, hostage, no more daily bloodshed while watching his friends die violent deaths. Every kiss from Lydia breathed life into Abram's soul. She slowly stroked his cock while licking his neck just how he liked it, both bodies looked so desperate for passion moving as if they were pressed for time. Abram's slight musky smell from all his labor made Lydia bow to her knees.

"Lyyydddia," They both stopped at once.

"Abram..."

"Shh," Abram cut Lydia off before she could utter another word. They both peeked around the barnyard, seeing if they could spot where Simon was yelling out for his wife.

"I will kill him now Lydia. It's time for us to be together," Abram whispered gravely. "We can flee from here. You know I am madly in love with you."

He needed to know what her answer was soon because he had been thinking of escaping into the deep dismal swamps that all the slaves on Planview would speak about. They spoke of how some had found homes there and security with the Powhattan. Secret folklores of the one who guides who he leads to the safety of the marshlands closer to the Chief Powhattan himself.

"I wants my Lydia, come ere' Lydia!" Simon had a whiskey bottle in one hand dagger in the other.

Simon was a remedial inbred slave. Low-life scum to the point of putting a knife to his own wife's neck to force her to have sex with him because she hated it so much. He didn't care he was a despicable experiment made by the European ways of human trafficking.

"I will kill him for putting his hands on you. He will pay Lydia; just say the word and I will do it!" Abram's eyes were full of fiery and love. A love that he yearned for when he said these words. "Then we can run to our destiny in the swampland. From there we seek help from the copper skin Seminoles I hear stories of the Pathfin..."

Lydia puts her finger over his lips, "I kno ya Abram but Simon is looking and rite now. I shall go back inside dey main house before he come outside with the field negros."

Lydia looked deep into Abram's eyes right before she turns to go back into the main quarters where he could never enter for any reason whatsoever.

"My love," Abram said breathlessly, staring as Lydia's bow legs and curvy hips go further and further away from his vision.

Abram began to come back to the reality of his daily routine. He was just getting over the wind chill and frostbite he endured during the potato farming and now he was assigned to tobacco and timbering for the increased transportation needs of. The growing Virginia agricultural industry. Abram would have to clear acres of land for Mr. Collins's tobacco planting, this would take intensive work. The men Abram worked with didn't talk much. Mostly cowards, they seemed to be scared to even yawn in front of a small group of white overseers that held whips and rifles. His day started at dusk soon as the sun peeked through the blinds of the clouds. He was there lined up with the other men waiting for the master to take them out with axes and hacksaws.

A part of Abram had given up on revolution, he had no army. He had no real plan to escape nor any idea about the landscape. Only stories from slaves that have been on this plantation for over 15 years in submission to enslavement with bodies full of master's whip lashes and hearts full of fear, fear that surpassed their fear of God himself. Or maybe their fear of God was manifested through their obedience to the pale skin slave master, his law was the only way they knew. His face was similar to the huge portrait of the white man they called, Jesus. They worshipped in Minister Quinn's church. One could only see the white man as a savior figure.

"Abram come here, over here Abram." It was Sarah.

Abram passed her shack every morning before timbering. "You shole should smile mo' ya' know Abram, you are so much mo' handsome when you sho' those big gums of yuurs,"

As Abram walked towards Sarah, he couldn't help but grin. Sarah was also so cheerful when seeing Abram, their connection had grown stronger. They developed that fresh off the boat, that's something they would never forget.

"Sarah save your jokes for when you need help hauling those sweet potato sacks from the fields," Abram grabs her waist pulling her closer to his chest. She laid her head there as he caressed her scalp, running his fingers deep into her roots. A serene silence followed, accompanied by deep breaths of codependency.

"Have you been practicing reading the book I gave you Sarah?" Abram asked with his eyes closed, feeling her response against the crease in his man breast with a big smile on her face.

"I'm trying but it's hard with the other slave women always watching and telling masa' everything. I try Abram, I try so hard," Abram felt her smile turn into concern.

"It's okay my Sarah, it's going to be ok."

Abram looked up at the sky an overcast had set in. He felt his wounds tingle as pulled away from Sarah.

"We have a long journey ahead to the west marshlands. Do you have any food to spare Sarah? I haven't ate in a few days beloved," Abram watched as Sarah walked towards the tinted-up shack. She came out with some bread and potatoes she had cooked over the skillet.

Abram took it very humbly. "Thank you, Sarah."

She nods with her eyes closed.

***

"Move out boys!"

Colonel Hitch was an old revolutionary war vet. It was said he was a British army deserter that sought out refuge on the outskirts of the swamp. He said there were too many niggers inside the swamp and the Indian niggers roamed the perimeter. He fell right into the huge demand for help among slaveholders who needed to keep a whip on the black laborers back. He rode that privilege, fitting right into dehumanizing a people for capitalistic gain.

Abram's group consisted of 25 black bucks as they were called. They walked 7 miles to the west of the swamp to do everything from chop trees to clear roads and dig canals. By the time these men got back to the Sendview plantation, they were too exhausted to eat. The labor itself was pure torture.

"Aye aye Abram my feet hurt like a summa bitch," said Theo. He was the youngest out of the men, a vibrant young man born an orphan. Said he was picking cotton soon as he could crawl being he was so black his skin looked purple depending on how the sun hit it.

Then there was Bojangle. He was a bonafide coward looking for every chance to tell the oppressor the plans of the slaves and anything else he could do to make it seem like he was on their side when truth be told he was scared for his life. Slave militias had burned his momma house after they betrayed his father, who was a scout for the American army until a white infantry soldier became jealous and accused him of being a spy for the British. They tortured him; it ended with his body being held by two horses on both legs while he was tied to a tree. When the horses were commanded to run, they took his father's limbs with them.

Abram was more infuriated with the fact Bojangle didn't want to avenge his father. He just laid down like a coward acting as if the white man was his friend. What was his definition of friendship? Tearing your black body apart while you're still alive limb by limb? The crazy thing was he kept a newspaper article about his Pa' as he called him and how proud he was of his Pa', who was killed and betrayed by the same men he submitted to, the same men that raped his mother to death after his Pa' was brutally murdered.

Abram would talk to Bojangle from time to time to examine him, to understand how his mind worked. Abram knew from his experience in war, a coward's fear can be easily manipulated. He knew a spineless man would do anything out of fear.

"Abram, I see you and Sarah ova der. I seen yaw."

Abram smiled as he walked the trail. "Focus on using that shovel boy. Today gon be a long day. What you got to eat up in that pouch there Theo?"

"Ooo I got some lemons and corn, Abram. Been hard finding some stuff, least till springtime come."

Abram picked up his stride. He saw Colonel Hitch looking back, "Hurry up here now Theo, that pale face is looking at us, how you suppose we get in that kitchen?"

Theo looked puzzled. "I mean I know we outside niggas but we could get some real good food to hold us through the last of the winter."

"Well yeah, Abram you're right. We shole could get us some sweet potato pie, fried cornbread, and some pig belly." Theo's mouth watered.

"See Sarah know some house niggas that could help us out it's just that cooking lady. What's her name, Theo?"

"Oh, you talking 'bout Momma Rae!"

"Yes, that's her name. The big lady," Abram responded.

"She shole can cook too." Theo instigated some more as he reached for his small flask filled with well water.

"Lady Rae cooks for the big house and Mr. Collins family and guests."

"Yes, she be cooking a mean pulled pork. They go crazy over her barbecue," Theo sounded excited like he was in there eating it with the family while knowing he was eating shitty chitterlings with the rest of the slaves.

"When you be eating from that kitchen Theo?" Bojangle was always fishing trying to get some information to report for fake admiration from white people.

"I was in the backyard one day, so hungry Lady Rae givin me-"

Abram cut Theo off quickly. "Bojangle why you asked so many questions?"

He looked back as they walked the trail. Bojangle paused for a second probably realizing his character flaw. "Isa habit I just be wantin' me some pok chops."

Theo let out an exaggerating laugh, "This nigga nosey as hell."

Abram continued. "Who's this man I hear about the blacksmith up close by the James River? He had was plannin to kill some white folks?"

Bojangle looked confused. Abram had kept quiet about being able to read, he'd seen the posters for the reward of Gabriel Prosser. He had rallied up the slaves for revolt on different plantations.

"He ah stupid nigga. He think he could kill masa' he had sum field niggas plans to murder masa." The vitiligo around Bojangle's mouth made him look like he had a permanent milk mustache.

"Seem smart to me. Who wants to keep living like this and gittin whipped? My lashes ain't never gon heal. I swear it hurt, got infected one time. The gnats keep getting in it when I slept turned my whole back yella and puss still had tah go out and pick cotton." Theo moves Abram's shirt. "Why you ain't got no lashes, Abram?"

Theo waited for an answer from Abram. He knew Abram was different and Abram was good at keeping his life a mystery. He was a master of deception, he learned being in war, to never declare war instead just wage it. Abram had to catch himself before he turned around to properly address Theo stopped in his tracks. A quick memory that he suppressed deep inside flashed in his mind. The young man he killed at The Battle of the Knives. The blood suddenly appeared on his hands as he trembled, he had killed many men but never a child that age around the same age as Theo. The orphan boy confined to this treacherous inhumane condition that he now accepts as his life.

Abram saw the boys' eyes as he stared into them. What was his name? How old was he? What made him want to be a soldier in the traitor mulatto army?

"Abram," Theo's voice made Abram take a deep breath.

"Because Theo, I was a house negro, I kept my mouth closed and minded my god damn business unlike you," Abram winks his eye at Theo. "Now let's keep up with the pack, you know Colonel Hitch will use that whip of his and I ain't getting no new lashes talking to yall niggas."

"Why you talk so proper?" Theo smiled as they picked up their pace. Abram always knew they didn't understand him or his past. Abram wasn't going to settle with his current position; he just didn't have an idea of how to escape it quite yet.

"Bojangle come herr up front with me," Abram said with authority. He lifted his pants leg all the up to the thigh. "That's where my lashes are.

The stab wound had turned keloid, or maybe here." He revealed his right shoulder a bullet that penetrated straight through.

Abram looked up ahead to make sure their huddle was secretive, Abram took off his shoe and showed them his foot, he could still hear the screeching from the rats chewing at his flesh.

"Them shoul ain't no lashes," Theo couldn't stop looking at the disfiguration of a man's foot, the flesh looked inside out.
He couldn't tell if the creased skin were veins or scars.

"All these wounds and none on my back because I stand and fight. I don't turn my back and run like a coward. These whites see my scars, they call us nigger but they're so arrogant they don't see my pain as a threat. My whole life has been about threatening with pain, enforcing the pain, enduring pain, like you yes, but always inflicting more pain on those who have tried to kill my father, my mother, my brothers I have always wanted revenge and I shall have it." Bojangle stood there confused. When Abram said father, he made sure to look Bojangle right in his eyes. Why didn't he want revenge like Abram? Was he scared? Fearful of what would happen if he was angry. Bojangle wanted to feel anger about his father but he was too panic-stricken. However, at that moment Bojangle felt anger he felt very different than he had ever felt before.

"Almost there," The Colonel called Abram to the front while sitting on his horse. "Abram, I got an extra piece of chicken if you can get these boys outta here in time for service over at Minister Quinn's church. Now that means we gone need to leave here sometime early before sundown ya hear?"

"Yes sir, Colonel," Abram smiled. "Let's get her done boys."

Colonel Hitch kicked his horse and headed further towards the marsh ravines to survey the area for the native Powhatan people. They hunted and had villages around the perimeter of the swampland. These were the peaceful natives; they knew nobody wanted to live in these swamps. Until they realized that the white man eventually would want every single thing he could lay his eyes on out of pure gluttony.

Colonel Hitch spotted another group of laborers further north he took a closer look. It was Bushrod. The man that inherited President George Washington's 40,000 acres of the swamp, after they had tried to exterminate the native tribes inhabiting the land just to drain it dry digging canals. Colonel Hitch signaled him closer, Bushrod's black stallion horse galloped aggressively towards his position, Colonel Hitch got off his saddle waiting for his approach. The massive beast slowed down next to the Colonel.

Bushrod was an English man. His mustache curled at the end and he was no more than 5'5. His napoleon complex came off very confident and he had a seriousness to him in conversation.

"Colonel Hitchy, how yah niggers holding up this winna?" He tightened his belt readjusting his whip. "I had a couple of my wretched savages hung up by James River followin after that Gabriel nigger. That one that was on the bounty list yeh. He got some foolish old house monkeys to try to plan an attack. He had some weapons, say he was a blacksmith. Can't believe no niggers knowing how to make no metal."

Colonel Hitch looked back in paranoia. "Yep, I saw the posters up around Sendview."

Bushrod pulled out his pipe and stuffed it with tobacco, trying to talk at the same time, "Say they was having meetin deep in this heer swamp up closer to Lake Drummond. Kno anything bout that soldier?"

People knew Colonel Hitch camped out by the swamp too along with the other deserter soldiers. "Well, those tree niggers, the Powmen warriors, they say the great spirit protects that there swamp. Those Indians let the runaway niggers in there. Some of em' even know the language paint they face up to. Hell, we couldn't even tell who was who sometimes. Shit was spooky up yonder Bushrod. I spent nights fighting off those coyotes and them damn black bears and those mosquitoes are big as fuckin bats in that place. I don't know how they survive deep in that hell hole."

Bushrod interceded after what seemed to be Colonel's deserter survival truths. "Since President Washington died, we been cutting down to the root of these marshlands and I been busy with chasing these niggers around. Between them trying to escape and the cotton gin, got the deep south begging fo' more nigger folk down there. But something got these savages stirred up I tell ya, even when my militias go hunting down in the Carolinas those Seminole niggers is causing a ruckus down there too."

"Colonel Hitch now, we gotta find out what's goin on around these parts. They scaring the woman and children 'round here. And them nigger Indians in there gone find out who's laying claims to this here land we need this timber and we have tah drain that Lake to do it. Anything in our way is dead."

"Dat right, Dat's right." Colonel quickly looked back at his workers. "Look here Bushrod it's been nice. I gotta get back to dem savages down there." Bushrod reached out his hand in a stern manner. "Any of those unruly beasts get out of control you put them back in line. We can't have no more of them Gabriel Prosser niggers comin out of nowhere now,"

Bushrod patted Colonel Hitch on the right arm before turning to mount his horse. Colonel Hitch stood there a minute, a case of nostalgia set it as he looked around. He petted his horse slowly.

"Whoa girl, don't wanna wake up those people in the swamp."

Colonel Hitch thought he heard something. He didn't mount his horse he just walked it down towards the slaves as he thought about Bushrod's demeanor as they spoke, maybe he thought he was a traitor but he wasn't there with him when his army left him for dead against the Americans. He had seen good men die. His hearing was damaged by cannonball fire, and his body weakened the freezing Virginia winters with no food. He saw men turn into cannibals eating corpses just to survive. Colonel Hitch had to suppress the sickening memories out of his head and what better way than to spend your days dehumanizing and devaluing black people. Being enslaved in his mind had led him down a path of being an oppressor himself. We all have our demons how they manifest themselves is a different story.

"Abram, make sure these boys clear this last acre here. Then we gon head on over to church before sundown I need me some Jesus in my life."

***

No complaints from a bunch of slaves granted half a day's work to attend church service. Especially when they could sit down while listening to Minister Quinn preach the gospel of Jesus Christ.

"Welcome. Welcome, all you uncivilized souls. This is Quinn's Ministries Protestant church. Yes, Jesus has blessed this American land of the free today. Shillings for the church are needed gentlemen, it is better to give than not to. And Colonel Hitch, make sure you seat your nigger beast in the back with the rest of those poor. Savages praise God. Thank you, sir."

The big sign in the church corridor said, 'Colored seats'. Abram read the words silently as Minister Quinn went back to meeting and greeting people at the door. The wooden floor creaked as all the members of the church begin to fill the wooden pews.

"This church is creepy," Theo said covering his mouth. "Look at the graveyard out yonda' Abram."

"I'm exhausted Theo, please spare me the antics."

"Antics? What does that mean? You know I ain't lying nigga. It smells like dead bodies in here," Theo said while holding his nose.

As they made their way towards the segregated section Abram noticed some people that looked like black folk, but they had feather necklaces with deerskin clothes and high cheekbones. Bojangle sat closer to the end of the pew while Abram found himself sitting directly next to a Native American. He had a hood over his head Abram could hardly see his face. The person's head stayed looking down into his lap as if he was praying. Abram started to say something when he glanced up at the front of the pulpit. He saw Colonel Hitch talking to a man that handed him a paper, he looked very concerned while they read the papers together. When they were down reading the scroll, they began to patrol the room looking over each row very thoroughly. Abram watched them as they served as security while Minister Quinn got ready to preach the evening sermon.

"What do you think they are looking for?" Abram asked the mysterious man sitting next to him as he kept his eyes on the two slave militia leaders scouring the room.

After he noticed there wasn't any response Abram turned to his left to find that the man was gone. He vanished; it was like he was never there.

"Abram come here boy," Colonel Hitch yelled across the room.

As Abram stood up, he noticed a Bible page ripped laying on the wooden floor where the mystical man had been sitting.

"Theo," Abram whispered while using his eyes to give Theo directions. "The paper."

Theo waited till Abram was moving in front of him down the pew towards the isle then slide it under his buckle shoe. As Abram walked towards Colonel Hitch, he was extremely nervous and confused. He was hoping he didn't seem suspicious as he made his way to him.

"Yesur," Abram said.

Colonel Hitch replied while squinting his eyes, "Did you see any funny-looking feather head niggers over there in that negger section?"

Abram hesitated. "No sir I can't say that I did. I mean we all ova' dere look the same tah me. It is the colors only section, sir."

The colonel stood there looking for a second, "Ok Abram but you keep ya eye out. Nobody has said much about it but some months ago Seke was killed on his damn plantation. Can you believe that? Whole thing went tah shit my slave army boys looking for a particular nigger. Mr. Collins mentioned you might know him. If you seen 'em you needs to speak up now. I like you Abram but I will hang you from a god damn tree like the rest of dese niggas, got me?"

It was all Abram could do to hide his smile, "Understood Sir." Abram nodded and headed back to his seat.

Minister Quinn began his sermon with a peaceful greeting.

***

Minister Quinn becomes more dramatic in his tone of voice, he lacked charisma and his growling resemblance to a troll made it worse. Abram almost throws up in his mouth disgusted by these colonizers finding any way to justify slavery. Even comparing it to being a blessing, saying it brought the slaves to Christ and civilized them, the nerve of these evil con artists and Abram looked up to see the people that looked like him shaking their head yes in agreement to the sermon. The colored people were embracing the message Minister Quinn was delivering.

"Weaklens," Abram whispered to himself. Abram then looked over at Theo. He winks at Abram.

Abram kept his eyes open; he was perplexed about the mysterious man's disappearing act. Was it Cezar? Couldn't have been his brother. And the Bible page, was it a sign? Some sort of letter from across the lands? Who helped Cezar kill Seke? Did Cezar kill Seke? Had to have been, his brother was the only person he could think of who would be brave enough to even try. All these questions rushing through Abram's brain, Abram had to admit it was satisfying hearing Cezar's oppressor was dead. At least Abram knew another plantation owner had met their fate but was Cezar alright? Did he need his help? Did that native man that sat next to him know Cezar?

Before he knew it all he heard was, "Amen."

Minister Quinn quickly reached for the shillings and pounds from the congregation, "Meet me outside. All of ya line up on the side of the church and wait for me we got somethings to discuss."

He looks at Abram and Theo making their way from the very back towards the narrow aisle leading towards the door.

"Hide it good Theo," Abram said as they walk.

"Don't worry Abram."

The men line up on the side of the church. They can see the old cemetery. It smelled awful and a slight fog floated over the headstones. Colonel Hitch came riding up with his stallion.

"Welp, it seems we have a nigger making trouble close to the Sendview plantation and we may have a bloody liar with us as well. Bojangle get over here." Colonel drops down from his horse. "You said you saw a man here Bojangle?"

Bojangle started to talk only to stutter out, "Yee, Yee, yes I did see a man sitting next to Abram for a short while then he vanished, Sir."

Abram became infuriated staring at Bojangle, he couldn't even look Abram in the eye.

Colonel Hitch pointed at Abram. "Is this true Abram?"

Abram replied, "No sir I saw no man, sir."

Colonel Hitch gritted his teeth in frustration, "Can anybody vouch for Bojangle's claim of seeing a man sitting next to Abram?"

Colonel walks up and down the line with his sword dragging the ground in front of the men. He stops at Abram and puts the sword directly under his chin, "Now I'll ask you again, did you see a man?"

Abram kept his eyes locked onto Bojangle. He wanted to kill him more than the man with the blade to his chin; Abram despised traitors.

"No," Abram said while staring the Colonel dead in the eyes.

"We'll see," Colonel smiled. "Let's head on back so we can better sort this out. Move out on my count."

Colonel swiftly withdrew the sword and reassembled it back into the case. Abram took a deep breath; he had held it since the blade was pulled on him.

Abram held his head up to the sky, whispering, "Eli, please guide me."

CHAPTER SEVEN

Redemption

"Come on now, we gotta hurry up and have dinner ready for Mr. Collins today. We can't be late, y'all don't want no lashing. Make sure the table is set and the apple cider is poured in the glasses you know Masa have to have his cider with his pork."

Lady moved with a sense of urgency in that kitchen, she had a whole pig smoking during the winter months. She kept at least 3 hogs to make it through in case bad weather hit. She kept the meat salted and preserved along with peach water and hard apple cider that Mr. Collins loved. Spirits is what they called the alcohol. For Scott Lady Rae made some mashed potatoes with an old remedy of deer jerky she learned how to dry and cure it from her aunty in South Carolina. She watched her in the kitchen before being sold further north to the Sendview plantation.

Mr. Collins saw her green eyes and it was love at first sight. She didn't hesitate on showing Mr. Collins her black girl magic in the kitchen and he was instantly hooked. Her voluptuous booty with dark freckles under each eye gave her a leopard print birthmark. Her thick hair was usually kept in cornrow braids straight back hung down between her shoulder blades. She stood out like a nigga in North Dakota. With natural glamour she had a firm demeanor about herself, and when she cooked she took pride in her meals.

"Hey Theo," Lady Rae spotted the boy lurking around the kitchen house looking for scraps.

"Yes mam," he said.

"You's ah seen Sarah round here?"

Theo pointed up the hill towards the barn. Abram was milking the cows and Sarah would sneak up there to see him at times.

"Shoulda known," Lady Rae said with a smile on her face.

Lady Rae made her way towards the barn. Sarah had missed some days of work. Mr. Collins informed her she was sick but Lady Rae knew better, especially with Abram laid up in that barn with his jaw swollen and a broken soul. Lady Rae could tell over the past couple of weeks things were a lot different with these two, they barely made eye contact with each other. When they spoke, they made sure one of them was doing work and they focused their attention on that which they were working on.

Lady Rae had never been raped by Mr. Collins so she looked at it differently. Lady Rae saw it as Sarah's fault. Had to have been something she did because Mr. Collins never treated her with any hostility. Of course, she got lashes for letting meat spoil or being late with the meals in the wintertime. But that was normal, she deserved that. She could understand why Mr. Collins did that to her. It was her fault too.

"Sarah, hey baby," the barn door creaked as she spoke.

"Oh, oh hey Lady Rae. I'sa coming, I was just."

Lady Rae cut her off, "I need you to fetch more taters. Sarah, please hurry hunny, it's almost dinna time and Mr. Collins havina some company ovah."

Abram gave her a stern nod, a nod as if to say you can do it.

"Here I come, bye Abram," both women waved at him, as he continues milking into the metal pail.

As the barn door closes Abram stops for a second, he reaches inside his boot and looks at the ripped Bible page.

"In the name of the Makendale let it begin."

***

Lady Rae and Sarah quickly made their way back to the kitchen house.

"Now Sarah I need yous to mash up dem potatoes now real good I got some herbs and spices, I'm serving up some good ole pork chops and mashed potatoes. I got some deer jerky fo' da boy along with some fresh Johnny bread,"

Sarah gave Lady Rae the side-eye, "I can't wait, Lady Rae, I'm so excited about the special dinner tonight."

"I have to go and see bout the dinin space in the house Sarah, can't be havin no mistakes tonight. Could you stay here and mash up those taters? Hold the kitchen down while I go up in the main house. Maybe I could find Mr. Collins while I'm up there and get his blessings on when to start bringing up the cider and fresh spring water."

Sarah wanted to grab Lady Rae by the neck when she mentioned that man's name while smiling with joy.

"I hope you find 'em dead," Sarah said to Lady while her face was twitching from holding back tears of anger.

Lady Rae sighs, "I know baby, but you has tah control yourself. We'd don't want you getting in no moe trouble okay?"

Sarah walks over to the pot, "You want these taters with butta' to?"

"Yes Sarah, I'll be back soon."

Lady Rae made her way up into the main quarters. She stops in the front room and calls out, "Mr. Collins, Lydia, Peter? It's Lady Rae here at the front door. Hello, Scott are you there?"

"Lady Rae is that you?" A soft voice said while peeping around the stairs. It was Mr. Collin's son, Scott.

"Ooo weeee look at you getting so big and strong like ya Pa."

He runs up to her full speed giving her a big hug.

"Awe Scott have you seen your father? I need to speak wit' him."

"He's in his room up yonda' talkin wit' Mr. Cary."

Lady looks around, "Okay Scott, let's gon down to the dining room then and see if the table is set."

Scott responds with a smile on his face, "I think the house niggas set up the table for supper time it looks real nice in there."

Scott took off racing to the dining room as Lady Rae followed behind. She always admired the paintings on the walls and the furniture along with velvet rugs laid so elegantly across the hardwood floors.

"Back here Lady Rae, in the pantry," Scott declares. The little boy didn't have a care in the world. Lady Rae noticed a new painting of a negro being lynched on the wall in one of the front rooms. There were families there celebrating death and the black body just hung there on a rope while they seemed to not even notice.

Lady thought to herself I wonder what he did to deserve that, did he have a family? Was his family there? How old was he? Maybe his family got lynched too, the painter who did this was very specific with each stroke of his brush Lady Rae could see his eyes bulging out of his skull, his neck clearly broken. Did Mr. Collins enjoy looking at pictures like this? Was this fine art?

It brought her even deeper into the world she tried to escape through cooking. But there was no escaping the truth, and the truth was that no matter how good she cooked or baked Lady Rae was a slave, a human that was purchased from a business ran by kidnappers. Kidnappers that not only stole your body they stole her way of life, her lineage, her everything. And if there was anything that was dear to you, they stole it from you and use it against you. She quickly snapped out of it heading into the pantry.

"Simon," Lady Rae had a tone like she was seeking approval. "Boys and gals gettin' dinner ready."

Simon was drooling all down his lips, being his remedial self.

"Ok Simon let me start fetching the food," Lady Rae turns to head out the pantry door. As she takes a step Simon grabs her arm.

Simon said, "bes make sure that food is good Lady Rae now gitt."

Simon left his mouth open looking into her eyes.

"Gon be the best suppa Simon you'll see," she said. Simon let her arm go slowly.

Lady Rae looks back at Scott and waves goodbye.

***

Abram sat next to the heifer with the Bible page in hand,

"H.E.M." Abram stopped reading the encircled letters on the page, he was startled by footsteps running near the barn.

He immediately stands up and walks to the horse stable.

"Theo I'm here," he said.

"I got it Abram, I got some good ole potatoes, and some skillet bread. I even got some dried pooke meat, umm hmm sho' did, I seen Lady Rae go inside masa' house and Sarah well, she seems alil busy so I grabs what I cuud!" Theo was excited.

"Are those apples Theo?" Abram saw another sack full.

"Yesuh some nice red apples," Theo said while taking a bite of one.

Theo had a fearlessness when he teamed up with Abram, he felt safe and protected. He did whatever Abram told him. Knowing he could get killed for his actions, his admiration for Abram exceeded his fear of white men. That's how Abram knew he could make a soldier out of him.

"Over here Theo, put those' rations over here under this haystack. Tonight, will be the night that defines yourself." Abram cracks his neck while holding his jaw.

"Gotcha good didn't he Abram?" Theo said in a sadden tone.

Abram looks him in the eye, "Sit down Theo I need to tell you the plan for revolution. This night will change your life forever. Are you ready?"

Theo nodded yes and responded, "But Abram what is revolution?"

Abram bends down on one knee to explain, "The note from Minister Quinn church was special, so special I didn't understand it for days until I summoned the ancestors. I was shown in my dreams, a man in Haiti dah distant land from which I came, where we fight white men for our freedom. The man had one arm; he had no sword but he was all-powerful, all-knowing in his everlasting teachings to others. The nature of him could bring life or death he was like the black Messiah."

He read Deuteronomy 32:32 out loud to Theo yet he still didn't understand the meaning behind the scripture. On the page there were letters circled. However, Theo knew nothing of those. Abram pulled back another haystack and revealed what looked like a string and a stick, the bow was also a new sight for Theo he had heard stories of Indians shooting flying Spears at white men but he had never seen one up close.

"Where did you get that Abram where da' arrows at?" Theo said with amazement.

"I ain't got none I stole this close to the swamp back by the trail we walk to clear the trees I wore that deer hide cloak Lydia gave me the old musty one it was. I hid it inside there. It was broken, I had to fix it best I could. The Indian people are with me. I know they are, I can feel them watching me, Theo." Abram shook his head as if to say nevermind, "I have killed many men, some with my knife, my hands but this saved me from sure death in my last fight this is the bow and arrow."

He pulls it back as if to measure the power of the weapon, Abram continues. "I have seen black babies fed to alligators, I've seen bodies on fire when the French came and took Haiti from the Spanish. I saw dogs eat men alive I fought with the best of men the greatest leaders Toussaint, Dessalines, and Moise. The revolution is a glorious change Theo, a change that made us equal men and standing for what you know is righteous. The only question you need to ask yourself is are you ready to kill for your freedom. It tis liberty or death from now on, or live your whole life as a cowardly slave picking at the white man's shit every day."

Theo's face shivered as he held back tears of emotions he never felt before.

"It's your choice Theo, liberty or death, it's your fuckin choice fre`."

Abram was breathing extremely hard standing over the boy, his speech made his heart jump. A sudden outburst made Abram hold his breath.

"I want to kill him so bad." Theo can barely get it out with the tears streaming down his face. "Peter takes my body; he takes it my me. Been doin it too long now I try to keep it out my head but I'sa can't sometimes. He ah devil man I want to kill em dead I swear..."

Before he could say another word Abram grabbed that boy and hugged him like he was his own son, he embraced him with a warrior's love then Abram jerked him back holding on to both his shoulders.

"Look at me Theo in the name of Ogun you will have ya' vengeance if you stick with me boy, you will live on forever as a symbol of bravery for the next boy or girl like you who made a decision of def over being treated less than a man. You kill for freedom and die with honor."

Theo looks up at Abram frightened at the thought of death. "Who is Ogun?"

"Just say it, Theo, say I am born free. Say I will have my free. Say I will have my vengeance. Liberty or death!"

Theo wiped those tears of hurt. He poked his tiny chest out and he repeated those very words that Abram said. And he felt rejuvenated he didn't even fully understand what liberty meant but it felt good saying it, it felt like the weight of the world was off his shoulders by being vulnerable with Abram and telling him his struggles with a despicable pedophilic cowardly piece of scum. Abram had become even more livid that not only was Peter a slaver but he was a homosexual child molester, stalking small black boys for self-gratification.

This is how Abram knew the evils of men were punishable by death. He suddenly understood why Jesus ran the Pharisees out the synagogues, he understood why King David and the great Prophet Muhammad were commanded to fight against the infidels. Some men just needed to be killed, Abram thought. All the volatile revelations to leave no survivors, to kill them all, the faith of prophetic men knowing they were outnumbered yet they still fought and they won. There was a thin line between spiritual guidance and capitalist genocidal gain. The colonizers understood how to make sense of their conquest and conquering by using both to their advantage.

"Tonight, I will have my revenge as my brethren across the seas are having theirs. I Abram son of Eli, soldier of mother Haiti will have my feast here in this land they call Amerigo."

"Shush," Theo puts his finger in front of his lips. "You huur dat Abram?"

Abram turned towards a small crack in the wooden board to see where the noise was, and what a sight he saw. It was Bojangle running away from the barn towards the main quarters. Both Abram and Theo looked at each other and raced to the barn door. Abram breezed through the wind after Bojangle, knowing he had to stop him before he got back to Mr. Collins and he would be snitched on by the traitor. Theo was right behind him, the sun was setting the crickets were beginning to sing, wasn't long before Abram realized Bojangle was slow or was Abram just that fast?

His war instincts seem to go into overdrive when needed. Abram was in soldier mode and this was the perfect training drill to prepare for the war to come. Abram tackled him hard to the grass, then he quickly applied pressure with a chokehold around Bojangle's neck dragging him back towards the barn, his heels dug into the earth as he was pulled. Closer to some nearby bushes out of sight from the nosey slaves lingering around the plantation.

"Theeeeooo! The rock there grab it!" As Abram choked Bojangle blue in his black and white vitiligo shaded face he knew what he had to do to make sure this boy was ready for what was ahead.

"Kill him, Theo! bash his fuckin head in kid!"

Theo stood there holding the stone, it was like time stopped. He was just crying his eyes out to Abram about being a rape victim now he is standing there with a sweaty palm gripping a heavy rock looking at someone with the same skin color as him but Theo was nothing like him.

"Do it, Theo! Kill him or Mr. Collins will hang us both," Theo started to strike then he hesitated. Abram had to convince him, "Do you want Peter inside of you again? Yeah, that's what you want ain't it so you want to be a victim your whole life or do you want free?"

Before Abram could say another word, he had a face full of Bojangle's blood from a powerful blow to the skull, then another to the forehead then the temple, then the eye socket. When it was done the rock sat inside of Bojangle's face like a bread basket. It was caved in so bad Abram cringed at the sight.

"Get his legs Theo. Come on, hurry over here behind the barnyard."

Theo kept losing grip from all blood on his hands and forearms. The smell, that smell Theo would never forget for the rest of his life. Abram had introduced him to murder. Theo had become a killer and barely knew why; all Theo knew he wasn't going to get raped anymore. He wasn't going to be laid down for a sick white man anymore. He was going to kill or be killed; besides he could hardly have a stool without bleeding half to death. The continuous encounters had made him suicidal but now he could kill the ones who were hurting and oppressing him instead of contemplating hurting himself. This made Theo feel empowered. He was finally finding what freedom meant to him.

They buried the body under some golden brownish leaves close to the bushes, there was no time to dig a hole. Revolution was here.

***

Sarah stood behind Mr. Collins at the dinner table, her armpits were sweaty, her mouth dry. She tried to swallow and her spit tasted like ashes.

"Gon git Mr. Cary some of that hard cider Sarah. We got tah treat our guest right on Sendview plantation. All my loans to expand my fields and get more horses came from this fella right here."

Mr. Collins was happy to have some company over. He was tired of dealing with Peter every day, he needed an escape. Besides, he knew Peter had deep dark secrets that he didn't agree with but who was he to judge. He was just as bad as he was.

"Ah now stop it, Mr. Collins, you know I just come to see bout Lady Rae and her pork belly," Mr. Cary gave Sarah the side-eye.

Mr. William Cary was a popular merchant around the Yorktown area, known to be close with bankers and a good translator of the Native American languages spoken by the Powhatan tribes. Most of the languages were disappearing along with the genocidal killing of the people but Mr. Cary had damn near mastered the Algonquian language. Being in tune with the people just to capitalize of the trades, learn the land the ways of the man and then use what you learned to steal it away from them, appropriation at its best. Mr. Cary was a businessman, in the business of exploiting human beings.

Sarah grabbed the flask filled with hard cider and went around the table and poured the liquor in each of their glasses, first Mr. Cary then it was Mr. Collins. Lydia sat beside Simon, towards the end of the table. Peter was smiling at Scott while he picked at his deer jerky and corn on the cobb.

"How did this lil brat get corn on the cobb? I want some of that not this ole mashed potatoes. I know ain't no Sarah made dem. She can't cook a lick." Peter and Scott laughed out loud.

Scott looked at his dad, "My Pa' like Sarah, he like Sarah a lot."

Mr. Collins looks over at Scott. Sarah softly interrupted, "I guess y'all don't want to taste the cream potato soup I made for our special guest Mr. Cary den?"

Sarah's soft yet sarcastic tone made all eyes land on her.

"Na, na, naw Sarah, I shoul' would like to try it," Mr. Cary said. "Wouldn't y'all like to try some soup?"

Mr. Collins takes another bite of the mashed potatoes on his plate, "Go get da gottdamn soup, Sarah."

Sarah checked everyones glasses as she walks around the table. Lady Rae had quickly brought out the soup and served everyone their bowl.

Sarah hears Mr. Cary asked Scott, "How you know ya Pa' love this nigga woman so much, Scott?"

Mr. Cary leaned in like a detective fishing for information. That's when Scott jumps up out his seat with all kinds of theatrics.

"Well, my Pa was in da barn pants down to here," Scott made a motion pointing down touching his ankles, "He was on top of Sarah breathing like donkey, heeee haaaw, heee haaaw. Den, den Peter hada rifle right at dat nigger while Pa' and Sarah was wrestlin' down dere in da barn yonder. Ain't that right Sarah?"

Mr. Cary chuckled after his performance. Sarah tried holding back her tears. She tried to show any emotional trauma, but she was tired she was hurt, she was empty like something was stolen from her soul and she couldn't get it back. The way Mr. Collins thrusts himself into her, choking her neck, her scratching at his forearm being dominated by devastation.

Her position of helplessness took form of just a lifeless piece of flesh being overtaken by the devil's dick stroking her body into a up and down motion that made her embarrassed to even look at Abram.

She shat herself, she remembered because the smell was gut-churning and that vandal of a man didn't skip a beat while staring at Abram as if he was smitten over him in some sick enthralled way. Getting off on another man's reaction while forcing his way into a woman's womb. Sarah didn't know if she was crying because Scott saw it or if she was enraged or embarrassed. She turned and politely walked away into the pantry room where she fell into Lady Rae's chest. Lady Rae consoled her, she was crying her soul out her whaling became louder and louder as the tears streaming turned her eyes turned dark red.

"I sorry Lady Rae." She looked her straight in the face as she whispered, "It's time."

Lady Rae looked at her with an expression as to say, *'time for what?'*

"Please excuse me. Have to go to the lady's room."

Lydia tells Simon something in a low tone as he eats with his hands, smacking his gums.

"Dammit Simon that's why we don't allow dogs at the supper table. Now quit all dat niggerish boy." They all begin to laugh at Mr. Collins's comment. "I be damned Lydia hardly ate any tators don't be wasting none of Lady Rae pork belly now."

"No, never sir, I needs the lady's room is all," Lydia replied.

"Gon get to the outhouse den but hurry back now. Lady Rae made some sweet bread for Mr. William Cary here, don't miss out."

"Yes Massa," she replies as she turns to leave. "Simon gon' wit her."

"Yessir," Simon gets up licking his fingers. "Scott come here boy," Mr. Collins said with a Stern look, his voice took a low pitch. Scott slowly walked around the table to the other side making his way into his father's lap.

"When did you see that what you said in the barn son?" Mr. Cary was listening closely for the story to unfold.

"I saw you Pa' you and Peter that night, I was scared alil' then Peter told me that's how we posed to treat niggers. He says one day I gonna have my own niggers."

Mr. Collins looked at Mr. Cary, he nods as to give him the go-ahead. "Son niggers is not humans like us, therefo' we can do as we please with dem. Your Pa' was just doing what's best for business ya understand son?"

Clearly, this is the only way to excuse such behavior. By downplaying your savage and animalistic ways was to project those same ways onto the real victims.

"Yessir," Scott smiles as his father rubs his shoulder.

Mr. Collins lifted his glass to the ceiling. "Let's make a toast."

Mr. Collins stood to his feet. Everyone follows in motion standing proud with their glasses high facing Mr. Collins as he begins his announcement. "I thought about my wife today, how proud would she be to see her son growin'. We owns all this land wit' plenty niggars to pick my cotton. He had a sinister smile on his face stroking his beard and mustache.

"Amen." Mr. Cary ad-libbed during Mr. Collins's short pause, "Hopefully my good ole friend Mr. Cary will see fit we continue to purchase the finest of niggers to work my fields. We do things differently down yonder. Soon as they clear out mo' of dem swamplands, we have our Acers."

Mr. Collins nods at Mr. Cary as to say, "Cheers."

Peter took a deep breath before he sipped. The glasses of water and cider on the table begin to slightly shake, the ground was trembling shifting the room. Mr. Cary quickly walks over to the dining room window and pulls the curtain back, everyone's heart dropped to the floor. Horses were running like wild mustangs out of the stables. The cows were scattered, running frantically across the cornfields. There was fire, fire that had spread so far across the plantation, you could see the size of the flame in the pupils of Mr. Cary's eyes.

"My God Mr. Collins," Cary was so in shock he began to lose his breath, he staggered back to his seat with heaving coughs and his face was Fresno pepper red down to his neck.

Peter runs over to him trying to aid him.

"Sarah! Simon!" Peter yells out, his voice came out shaky, he was terrified.

The fire was spreading, getting closer to the house. Scott was frozen for a long moment. Not knowing what else to do, he hid under the table.

"Mr. Cary, hold on! I'm here," Mr. Collins said while holding him upright in the chair.

He turned his head to the sound of Peter in the corner of the room projectile vomiting on the floor, nearly choking on his tongue. That's when Mr. Collins realized something was wrong, something was seriously odd about this. With sudden realization, he knew they had been poisoned, this was part of a plan. Mr. Collins caught his balance on the back of Mr. Cary's chair trying to stand up. He was beginning to feel dizzy and suddenly very weak. He stumbled into the pantry door where Lady Rae was panicking herself trying to seeing the blaze and coughing from the smoke.

"You poisoned us you lil wench," Mr. Collins lunged at her grabbing her throat strangling her with the strength he had left.

Lady Rae gasping for air was trying to tell her master it wasn't her, that she would never. From behind a hand emerges clutching a long saw blade. The hand forced the blade into Mr. Collins neck, right on the soft spot. The blood gushes out of the slash in his neck as his grip loosens and he slowly drops to the floor blood seeping between his fingers as he holds his neck. Lady Rae sees Sarah still crying holding the knife now dripping with blood.

"This is what you were cryin fo? We all gone die now. You done lost your damn mind child."

Sarah stands there for a second whimpering, "Burn in hell with em den."

Sarah sprints out the door with one person in mind.

"Abram..." she said while holding up her dusty raggedy dress.

"Heeellp!" It was Scott screaming stuck somewhere in the flaming house.

Sarah stopped abruptly. She was coughing so much she couldn't breathe; her eyes were burning from the smoke.

"Scooott!" Sarah knew she had to leave now, there was no turning back for him.

Sarah ran towards the front door; it was engulfed in flames. She tried covering her face, searching for an escape. Sarah found the window, barely being able to breathe she slipped through the window falling to the ground outside about to cough up a lung. Her part was done; Sarah had kept her word to Abram for revolution while he almost burned her to ashes. Her eyes were streaming tears, she laid there on the grass and listened to all the chaos, all the slaves on the plantation screaming for help.

The cries of devastation gave Sarah goosebumps. The floors of the house were collapsing. She needed to get up and find Abram and Theo.

"Come on Simon git up now," a woman's voice comes through the mist of loud coughing.

"Lydia!" Sarah moves towards the voices.

As she did, she heard a commotion from her rear. With her vision blurry, she saw a man and young boy on horseback stopping a few feet from Lydia and the man barely hanging on to life.

"Lydia we must go now befo' Colonel Hitch gets back. The tree line is set ablaze, I have enough food to lasta week's journey," Theo looked back at Sarah.

"We will ride as far as this horse will take us, deep into the forest towards the swamplands. Lydia my love, leave him, let us get free."

Abram reached his hand out for his love while stepping closer to her, yearning for her, finally he could be complete in his quest for love. Lydia reached out with her hand but not to grasp Abram's hand. Lydia snatches Simon's pistol out of his waist, she raises the flintlock at her supposed soulmate.

"Yous killed my husband, Abram. Yous...yous, killed everybody in massa' house. There's no life out there in those woods Abram. "Lydia was delirious. She was in shock. The chain of events had made her realize she wasn't truly ready to be free even if she loved Abram's touch, his cock, his muscular stature his romantic way of painting a picture of perfect love outside of this plantation.

She now saw it was only perception, an image of what could be. She never believed in his vision she just fell in love with an idea, folklore of slaves escaping and fighting or even killing for their freedom. It was all just foreplay, making the love affair itself an escape and that was more than enough for her.

"Lydia plea-please don't do this I warned you bout the revolt, and from the poison. I saved you so we can be together so we can be free."

Lydia looks down at Simon, "Yous ah killer Abram. What about my babies on this plantation? How will dey live wit out me or massa' around to feed them and cloth dem?"

These kids barely knew her, she resented them from birth because she was bred like a dog. She wouldn't have known if some of them were still on the Sendview plantation or sold to the Georgia borderline. The pistol was shaking. She was confused and Abram realized he had fallen for a woman that had never even known herself.

"Goodbye Abram," The gun sound echoed loud, the flash startles Abram but it was too late. The bullet pierced his flesh the blood projectiles out the exit point sending the stallion into a frenzy running off into the woods. Abram felt his body flying backward, heard Theo and Sarah screaming, running his aid as he hits the ground. Lydia had shot him for destroying her reality. The same reality she had lied about wanting to leave behind. The lashes on her back, the punishment on her womb, the rapes and demoralization she suffered since her eyes hit the light coming out of her mother's womb. She was sold like a piece of delicate merchandise because even tho nobody wanted damaged goods, they still will find a way to get their money's worth out of their purchase. This was the only life she knew. She could not imagine a life without the white man.

"Yous wretched bitch!" Sarah ran full speed past Abram's motionless body on the ground. She jumped Lydia's back as she tried to run away, choking her so hard around her neck it looked like the veins on her temple were about to burst out of her head.

Her rage outmatched Lydia's struggle to pull loose Sarah wrapped her legs around Lydia's waistline. She didn't waste time, she squeezed harder until she felt her breathing stop completely. And when she did, she kept choking her and choking her until she heard her neck crackle. Theo was on both knees screaming.

"Abram, Abram! Open ya eyes!" Theo applies pressure on Abram's upper chest, the blood flowed in between Theo's fingers.

Theo knew the smoke could be seen for miles; it wouldn't be long before Colonel Hitch saw the plantation set ablaze they were running out of time. Abram felt himself shivering like he was freezing going into a panic attack while holding Theo's hand gasping for air. The sound of his voice faded. As Abram sank into a hole of blackness, he began to float through it lost, glossy flickers of light flashing like lightning through a drifting blue mist that appeared randomly in this place Abram found himself.

***

Faint sounds circulated in the dark matter. The space he was in felt woeful as if he was in the very darkest place of his soul. More random cries of different voices filled the crepuscular black shaded atmosphere. This place was truly the bottomless pit of pure nihility, he wanted to weep but there was no real empathy, only self-penalty of being in a dark chamber where the muggy blackness is so strong around you it felt like fog. Was this oxygen? Abram didn't even know if he was breathing. Though it felt like a part of himself. Somehow, he didn't know his purpose.

"What happened to me?" Abram said to himself. It seemed as if he was only a fragment of conscious thought passing by the other side of the veil.

More connected to something bigger than himself. Like he was a cell in the blood as it flowed through a universal body. He had dove into a pitch-black abyss of total sorrowfulness, knowing you had not received the judgment he deserved yet, but it was coming.

His soul was dwelling in a gloomy lagoon of dark shrouded secrets of the inner being. As the sound moved all around him, he felt what seemed to be his limbs turning into wings. Still not able to see the dark fog, he could feel something shapeshifting inside of whatever vessel he had transitioned into. Through the blue mist a thin line of light began to appear. The more the light came closer the more Abram felt as if an unknown source was manipulating this place like a simulation. He felt indestructible yet so helpless at the same time. He just submitted to the will of whoever was directing these changes into a blacken crystal ball of mystical existence or nonexistence he had no clue.

The light drew closer forming into what matched the form of a system of stars like constellations. But these were not stars. More like circles of energy with intelligence, with a frequency that could speak to you without actually speaking. The circles of energy engulfed Abram with an overwhelming force, making him see through his third eye. The dark matter split, a metamorphosis of what looked like time passing by with different aerial views of Abram's life flaring in front of him. Then finally he felt himself, he was on the coast. Looking down at a trail of blood on top of the white sand beach. He followed the blood. The further he got down the stream of blood the closer he got to a body lying there stiff. A ray of light beamed down on this person the blood gets thicker as he walked up.

The walk was more like a hovering feeling. Abram made it to the body lying there. The person's face was disfigured so bad he couldn't tell who it was. Then it was like somebody turned on the audio to a motion picture film. Crowds of white men cheered and shook hands with African men in some sort of harmony, glorifying what had just happened to this body.

"What happens to this little one?" A man wearing a cross and a long silk woven robe is pointing at Abram. His face is camouflaged deep inside a hood his face impossible to see.

From a short distance, that now seems to have a huge ship in the background with cannons on each side, the flag was unforgettable. It was stuck in Abram's conscious and that's what Abram felt like. As if he was just a mobile notion of vision examining his matrix decoded. The red and green with a crown cloth ripple through the wind, the man wearing the cross-hand seemed like it belonged to a giant. Everything was so vague however somethings were exemplified with much detail. A loud horn sounds so loud Abram covers his ears. He could see the sonic waves moving in midair. The feeling of hallucination took over the scene, making everything happening continue at a slow pace.

The man wearing the cross directed his attention to a woman hollering at the top of her lungs, Abram could see her mouth moving but couldn't hear her saying anything. She ran towards him and the body lying beside him kicking up sand as she sprinted towards them yelling frantically.

"Mutter," Abram said out loud.

He was deaf; he couldn't hear his voice or the noise from the horn had pierced his eardrums. He remembered his mother clearly now, what happened to her. How they took her on that huge ship. Men violated her, pissing on her while ripping off her clothes. It seemed like this was some sort of vindictive placement of humiliation towards his parents, but why?

Abram's mother looked directly at him and said, "Dese men killed Eli."

Abrams eyes filled with tears but for some reason in this realm he couldn't cry. Fighting in the grave with death, but was he dead or alive? This had to be death, dwelling in the repeated shadows of himself. The tears made his sight blurry, everything faded. He wiped his eyes in what felt like a slow manner. That's when everything turned back to the blacken fog, a thickened smoggy substance he swam through. The glimmers of lightning began to reappear, a feeling of being spun around came over Abram. He was dizzy as if he was blindly caught up inside some sort of a cyclone. Abram's consciousness was opened again, this time it was like he could see only through his own eyes.

He had no vertical vision, or peripheral, only straight ahead. Something was heavy in hand it was a sword; the blade was shiny chrome perfectly crafted ridged edge with serrated teeth at the end of it. Abram held it in front of his visual then. He lifted to the sky with a motion of what seemed to be desperation. The sword ignited with a blue flame the fire lit up the whole atmosphere. hHe was consumed with a feeling of empowerment and godly strength. As Abram looked straight, he could see an army forming against him, hundreds of them.

His sword was still covered in flames as he stood there, he felt no panic, no adrenaline rush. His thirst to kill had been constrained as the army got closer, the threat began to make a circle around Abram and his sight was limited to only looking forward. He could feel the circle's circumference enclosing on him, the flame on his blade started to diminish. As the bodies got near to him they looked like silhouettes of human beings without features or colors.

Out of the black, each face came forth, "Why did you kill me, Abram?"

The voices became surround sound asking repeatedly, "Why? Why Abram?"

Each of the faces faded the black, in and out, repeatedly. Whispers of murdered men were what made Abram who he was, a warrior. He had to accept his actions, he had to see every person he had killed.

He couldn't respond to them all, and even still in this nightmarish spine-chilling place his inner being screamed out, "LIBERTY OR DEATH!"

***

Colonel Hitch held his bullwhip in one hand and flintlock pistol in the other. He looked down from the hilltop at the Sendview plantation with his face twitching from carnage taking over his nervous system, the slave patrols were with Bushrod to the right of him. He chained the slaves that accompanied him on the daily routine toward the dismal swamp. The smoke and screams of bloody terror traveled for miles. He headed back soon as he heard them in a panic knowing something had to be terribly wrong, the sight made him cringe.

"I got militias and continental army men on march ya heer Colonel?" Bushrod looked straight into Colonel Hitch's face one hand on his pipe the other gripped to his sword on his hip.

He was livid, beads of sweat dripped on his forehead and nose. "Gon have to round up these niggers to, I reckon Mr. Collins is dead along with..."

He paused.

Bushrod finished his sentence, "Scott."

You could hear the pain in Colonel's voice. "Let's move now can't wait for those troops Bushrod if there are any survivors, we gots to move now to save 'em."

Colonel Hitch mounted his horse as he looked back at the slaves, he had chained, "Stay put yous savages. May gawd have mercy on your sorry souls."

In all they were about 17 men strong, verily no one man could cause this much disarray on such a large piece of land. The men were expecting a group of runaway ravaged slaves thirsting for the white man's blood. They moved closer to the plantation. Most of Bushrod's men scanned the perimeter with rifles pointed. All the cows, chickens, horses, and pigs were running wild. Some slaves remained in their shacks, others stood around the main quarters staring at the fire as it engulfed the house. Bushrod and Colonel Hitch dispersed the men as best they could, trying to gather the animals and round the slaves back into their run-down huts. The men treated the farm animals with more respect than the slaves.

The soldiers were whipping the women. They pushed the children to the ground interrogating them yelling, "Who did this? Who killed Mr. Collins? Where's Scott?"

They couldn't go inside a burning house to save anyone, so they took their revenge out on any black body they saw. Colonel Hitch moved around hysterically, hoping to see any sign of the boy. The night was settling in, to the east side of the plantation he saw what looked like a group of men. He couldn't get a good view to confirm the glare from the flames and heat waves coming off the house made it hard to pinpoint. Maybe it was the militia that Bushrod mentioned marching to meet him at the rendezvous. Whoever it was, Colonel felt something unsettling from the movement of the figures in the distance. The horse was pacing back and forth, that's when Colonel saw a torch being lit, one after another until the whole eastern treeline resembled a Christmas tree.

He tried to spot Bushrod from his telescope to get a closer look into the direction of what looked like an assembled small army of men. Colonel needed to identify who this was quickly, to plan their next move if nearby tribes sensed any vulnerability on the plantation all hell could break loose. A soft cough from closer to the porch caught Colonel Hitch's ear. "Someone dere?" Colonel stopped to listen. Another suffocating cough came again from what sounded like it was below his ear. Colonel kept low listening for any response, his body language was despondent as he tried to keep hush and move through the debris and smokey fog that surrounded him. Only glares of light he could see but he couldn't see too far, Colonel Hitch knew then he was a vanquished man but he couldn't show it. He had to keep going, keep killing and enslaving people to uphold power. His conquest wasn't ending anytime soon. At least that's what he felt like as the soot and black smoke filled his airways.

"Scott? Is tha, tha' you boi?" Before Colonel Hitch could reach his arm out to save a survivor, a native war cry filled the smoggy area and screeched the ears of Colonel Hitch. He whispered to himself, "Oh no, not now."

***

His hands were bloody. Chief Wuhonee wiped them on his bearskin breechcloth. He had arrows to his back wrapped around his long torso. The width of his chest made it a good fit. Wuhonee held a torch in his bloody right hand the flame came closer to his face as the blood dripped onto the dark brown hair of his stallion's back, the horse's eyes bulged out the side of his head.

"Whoooa," Chief Wuhonee said in a low voice.

The complexity of their trauma bond was connected by perfidious intentions. Both were very unpredictable, loose cannons as they say. They had enjoyed spoils of war and pillaged. There were so many villages that calling it a war crime would be an understatement. Wuhonee tied his ponytails back behind his head, disregarding the blood that reeked off his fingertips. The paint on his face and horse matched; dark burgundy coated the chest and front legs of his ride, with bright yellow stripes across both sides of the horse's front legs.

Wuhonee took a deep breath through his broad nostrils, so broad many would mistake him for a black man. It made no difference to him, anyone standing in his way was a dead man, woman, or child.

Chief Wuhonee was the leader of the cottonmouth clan, a renegade clan that sent fear through the white man's heart for decades in the eastern regions of Virginia's coast. When the pilgrims and colonists first landed in Virginia and met the Powhatan in peace, the settlers spoke of an Indian alliance on wild horses that would come ravage the settlements burn the campsites kill the farm animals, kidnap the children, and rape the women. But most gruesome of all tales was the narrative of the dog soldiers. These men would chop the limbs of people into pieces while leaving them with gashes in their flesh that looked like what some say were bites or gouged flesh to the bone, mostly the small children.

This spread a horrifying rumor that the children's blood was so sweet that they craved it, so the dog soldiers would feast on the nectar of the youthful loins. An early settler of Jamestown had a diary that was found written in Dutch and translated into these dreadful stories of unbelievable sights that the British put off as lies or hysterical thoughts describing a savage Indian Chief that would appear in the night with a painted face and horse with soldiers that seem to move like dogs that even the wolves and coyotes stopped howling when in their presence of a fully illuminated moon. There were tales of the Chief's brown stallion that would stay behind after the ambush to eat the remaining flesh of the corpses ripping tissue from bone. However, the stories were put off as mythological writings, a flesh-eating horse?

No way. During the cold Virginia winters when the settlers actually became cannibals themselves. But the British and Continental American army and militias knew better, they always knew there was some truth to the stories of the cotton mouth clan. Chief Wuhonee signaled for his dog soldiers to encircle the plantation. Before he assembled his bow he reached in his bag and grabbed a bloody skull. His army had just removed the heads of the Virginian slave militia that Bushrod had assured Colonel Hitch was the coming reinforcements. In a state disarray, dispersed like prizes to each dog soldier in his army. It was like the limbs of the men they killed empowered them with immortality. One of Wuhonee's commanding soldiers drew his sword as he looked forward; the torch flame disappeared inside his pupils. The dog soldiers were on the hunt.

"Naz-tsaid, (kill)," Chief Wuhonee said lifting his bow pointing to the fire.

All seventeen men ran full speed towards the burning plantation. Chief Wuhonee and two of his generals stayed slowly striding behind the killer army on their horses and listened as screams of agony floated through the smokey night air. Bushrod and his small platoon started firing shots, the dog soldiers flanked the men giving them the advantage.

"Fall back," Bushrod yelled as the dog soldiers shot arrows at the men from what seemed to be out of nowhere. The men who were hit grabbed the arrows trying to pull them out of their flesh.

The dog soldiers knew how to strike, they were in sync, like a pack of wild hunters that had experience like poachers, killing without reason besides petty gain. Bushrod managed to find cover behind an old shack. As he peeked around the corner towards his injured men, natives were moving in closer and closer. He could see how they walked slightly crouched over throughout what was left of the light of flames from the main quarters. Behind him he heard something moving, it was pitch black toward the woods now he couldn't see anything, yet he could feel movement approaching. From out the bush, some shadowy figures moved slowly looking around them making sure the area was clear.

Bushrod didn't move and he held his breath until he saw the figures more from the light of the house fire, that's when he witnessed it for himself. He saw these beasts of men salivating at the mouth so much it was dripping off their chins, the foam-like saliva made them look. Inhuman the shocking sight made Bushrod gasp for air. Almost shedding a tear, he didn't want to watch these cotton-mouth savages eat the fallen men alive. His heartbeat was vibrating his entire body, Bushrod slowly gripped his hand around his sword he would surely die before he sat and saw his men be eaten alive by dogmen. He would make his stand now by himself he would muster up what bravery he had left. Both his hands shaking from the fear of death.

He made a choice to die and be devoured with his men. As he stood the earth moved with him rumbling beneath his feet, then there was a silence, so much he heard the crickets chirping, he cherished the sound. That silence was suddenly overcome by another noise, the night sky lit up like fireworks. The Continental Army trumpets were high in volume. The cannonballs bursting in air gave light to a flag with fifteeen stars, red and white stripes ten feet up in the air. Bushrod looked astonished as the artillery brightened the night's sky. The natives scattered back in the woods as some of them were caught by the bombs that landed across the plantation. Some of Bushrod's men flew up in the air from friendly cannon fire. He quickly tore his undershirt tying it around a tree branch he had to wave a white flag towards the army for them to cease firing.

Bushrod ran full speed into the crossfire, he was getting closer. He tried to raise the flag higher for the soldiers to see. As he frantically ran, he stumbled and he fell over, dropping the homemade truce sign knocking himself damn near unconscious. The cannon fire ceased followed by soldiers yelling, horses neighing along with the suffering screams of fatal injuries.

Lieutenant Goldman smelled of a musky bloodhound. Half his face was burned off, his damaged skin was peeled back to his ear stretching his smile. His men obeyed and respected their commander, Goldman was a highly skilled officer from God knows where. Some speculated if he was a British army deserter that reverted to the new American legion of democracy. During these times there was no way to know how high-ranking soldiers got their stripes or how many men they killed or battles that fought in. It was all about American expansion and the brave men willing to pledge allegiance to that star spangled banner.

Some infantryman even doubted Goldman was even his real identity. His claims of taking up arms with General Washington to naval service with John Paul seemed so robotic like he was born to kill and led those willing to do so. Lieutenant Goldman's Jewish background gave off the impression of a missionary for hire, a type of feel as if he could wear many faces just to mask his real one. At least before it was halfway blown off by cannonball fire.

"Time for some intel. This man has to know what happened."

CHAPTER EIGHT
The Southern Ground Railroad

She followed the smoke trail. The cannon fire echoed for miles and miles bombs were vibrating the land along with rifle fire. *Men of war,* Konah thought to herself. All white men want is war and bloodshed so much energy put into the sword, so much put into conquering, and owning other human beings. Her mind wandered off. She regained focus her feet were like feathers moving through the dead leaves and tall brush in the forest. She had to move quickly; time was running out. Revolution was now and she knew her purpose was to help guide the strongest fighters in the right direction. She knew the way, the rivers, every pond, and the lakes in between plantations. She found her way with her ears as much as her eyes, listening to the echoes of night owls and crickets to help guide her way. The moonlight was in and out due the cloudy overcast that advanced close to the Virginia treetops.

Konah tightened her bag and gripped the crystal on her necklace her heartbeat was rapid with waves of anxiety impacting every step in the dark woods. A horse neighing caused her to turn her head suddenly towards the commotion. It was a dark horse. Konah spotted the thick mist of breath coming out the animal's nostrils. As she got closer Konah saw the saddle, she approached slowly making a smacking noise with her mouth trying to get the beast's attention.

"Easy there," Konah reached her arm out cautiously hoping to mount the horse. She stopped about six feet away. "Calm down now I won't hurt you none, ya see?"

Konah tried to touch the horse's head, a strong swing of the horse's neck startles her, "Wooa ,wooa, nah."

Finally, she's able to pet her neck. That's when she felt the blood it was thick on one side up the ear. "Are you hurt gurl?" She looked for injuries on the horse. "Tis is not your blood is it? Still warm..."

Konah needed this horse to get closer to the smoke trail. Screams that sounded like women wallowing in sorrow and men grunting in pain. The voices carried over the mist into the cool wind. She needs to get closer to the treeline Konah thought.

"Dey should be there," Konah's sarcastic grin made her nerves settle as she rode closer to the sounds of sorrow. What did she mean, they? Had she foreseen this happening? Or maybe it was Sparrowhawk making his reappearance after recovery. It was time to get to the bottom of this.

***

The Sendview tree line

Tears flowed down the crease of her breast like a clear fresh spring waterfall. Sarah looked at Theo, his hands dripped with blood. Some stained his upper lip as he wiped his nose.

"Deres' blood everywhere. My god help us please, please don't die Abram we need you please!"

Theo could hardly watch Sarah crouched down crying so intensely. It was so terrifying, he was in total shock. As he stood there he started to focus on his breathing; he flashed back to Bojangle. How Abram made him smash his head in with the rock. How in some sick scandalous way he felt numb, but more of an emotionless numbing, rather than the kind that came with preparing to commit depravity. Seeing death or murder does something to a man that is unexplainable. If you have blood on your hands or had seen homicidal acts, it lingers in your soul causing you to constantly fight the trauma and memories that come with it. You develop a sense of immorality whether you realize it or not because you played the role of god by taking a human's life.

"Sarah!"

She was still weeping out loud.

"Sarah!" Theo said again. A stinging slap across her face brought her attention towards Theo. "Grab his legs."

Theo wraps his arms under Abram shoulders. One of them is soak in blood so he had to squeeze tighter, "We draggin' towards the tree line maybe we can fine dat ole horse somewhere close to dem woods. Dat slave patrol here, I heard dem white men chasin dem niggas round dat fire. Dem natives round here too. I knows dey is. I heard dat weird noise from across the way dere yonder."

Sarah didn't care to know what Theo was saying through all that heavy breathing, struggling to drag a two-hundred-pound man to cover.

"Stop please Theo. I need a break. Abram is leakin out again, ya needs tah help him now! Theo do sumn please!"

This was the most desperate he ever seen a woman, Theo looked into her tearful glossy eyes. "Okay nah Sarah, check inside his muf is he bleedin in his muf?"

She examined his mouth moving her two fingers around about his tongue.

"No," Sarah responded with urgency.

"Ok nah hold his head up nah." Theo had to apply pressure on Abram's chest so he just sat on the entry wound. "Dis should stop the bleedin but Sarah, we needs some water could you gets to the wale?"

"The wale on the other side of the fields up yonder?"

The sound of leaves ruffling in the woods froze their thoughts.

"Who's dere?" Theo tried to deepen his voice.

A heavy breath from the horse's nostrils comes next, Sarah smacks her lips. Walking towards the sound as she gets closer to the woods, she sees a glare of light through the thick bush.

A hissy raspy voice asked, "Is that man Abram?"

Sarah is stunned looking back at Abram's body, his chest was barely moving up and down filling his lungs with air.

"I am Konah, I save his friend Cezar. We were on the Seke land across the York River. But these men no slaves."

Theo looks conflicted, wondering where this strange person had come from. The feminine voice answered as if reading his mind. "I follow the smoke trail all the way here, I hear the gunshots. The cannon fire brighten up the dark clouds these must be meant for me to guide him."

Theo begins to speak back until Sarah interrupted him, "Hush." Then Sarah asked, "This man Abram, what land is he from?"

Konah paused before she answered she looks up to the sky holding the crystal around her neck. "Haiti, he is from the land of freedom."

Sarah falls to her knees with joy half giggling as if to say, *God you are really something*. Konah steps outside the cover of the forest so they can see her completely. Her appearance was mystical, dark brown skin seemed to absorb the moonlight while reflecting a glowing layer across her face. Her large eyes baring hardly any white seemed black in the night, on a pleasant face with long eye lashes and full lips. Konah's body was slim, fit but trustworthy because her scars on her body told a story in itself.

"We mus hurry, I hear the dogs. I knows a place, tie Abram up on dis horse."

Theo replies quickly "She shot em! That stupid wench shot him. He's hurt bad. We needs a torch to see-"

Konah stopped him mid-sentence while looking at Sarah, "No, no light. We use the moon. The night sky is clear I have already called on the dark angels to help us get dere close to the streams there is a cave I can help Abram, I was meant to help Abram you mus trust me."

Sarah found the hissing in Konah's voice to be sincere. Besides, what other choice did they have?

"Wat is ya names?" Konah asked while reaching in her bag.

"Sarah, and dis is Theo. Abram free me. He show me how to poison those wicked people while he set the whole plantation ablaze. They will surely hang us and have our heads on a stake."

Konah stopped what she was doing to look into her eyes, "Yah say Abram?" Konah said trying to confirm once and for all. Then replies "They will neva' have that pleasure and ya journey has jus' begun. Sarah, your bravery warms the hearts of the ancestors." Konah becomes more urgent now. "Theo, spread dis along the tree line and up the field a bit."

It was gunpowder. Konah was trying to cover their scent. She knew the slave mobs with dogs would be on their trail soon.

"I am the south trail. I am the Pathfinder Abram spoke bout that kno de way down Gullahs. I kno de way to true freedom," Konah had to explain quickly what was happening, "Sarah, I da one who gave Abram de hemlock poison plant to start a revolution here. You part of it now. You help us get to the south trail to true independence and we have an army dere. We must go south and follow the Southern cross."

Sarah was shocked, so this little woman was behind this?

"I thought niggas ran north. Look at the north star it shines bright tonight we can follow it."

Konah watches Theo as he spreads the gun powder on the ground around their scent, "No child, the north is dangerous, can't trust those white folk dere so much right now. Our people have land in the Gullahs along the swamp ravines, some British are dere. We have allies' wit de red stick natives and creeks against de wicked men. We grow crops in watermelon towns. We have lands and we have armies ready to fight for dere families."

Konah had such conviction saying this to Sarah she didn't hesitate to embrace her energy. At that moment Sarah realized her destiny was deeper than she could ever imagine. "Only a select few can go into the Gullahs wit me and I chose you Sarah. Get free with me."

***

Colonel Hitch hugged Scott tight in his arms. He was relieved to know the little boy survived the massacre. They waited under the rubble for the flames to slow and battle to end. It seemed like forever for the gunfire to stop. Scott kept thinking about death. He would do anything just for it to stop. All the pain, all the killing, all the terror. Most of all to be back with his Pa'. His dad was dead burnt to ashes by a wicked black devil man. He couldn't understand how a man could do such evil and vile things without a conscience, after all his Pa' was a good man, right?

Mr. Collins looked after his niggers. He made sure everybody was fed, he kept food and clothes on their backs. Although it was to the expense of the blood, sweat, and tears of the free labor from the American negro. His Pa' did not deserve this, it was all too much for a child to think about. It was unbearable for anyone to think about. Something had to be done about this. Trauma quickly turned to anger, Abram's face began to appear in his head, Sarah's voice began to echo in and out his eardrum.

"Scott, hey Scott look at me boi. Who did this? Tell me what went on?" Colonel Hitch had tears in his eyes. The man's glossy eyes were contagious as Scott burst into tears as well.

Scott began to tell Colonel about Abram. How he started the fire and Sarah helped him. Scott never thought Sarah was evil enough to help kill his father. "She poisoned the food but she may sho' I ain't gets me no potatoes jus some corn on the cobb my daddy and Peter had the mash taters."

Colonel Hitch looked a bit puzzled, "One dem niggers poison dem boi?"

Scott shook his head, "Dere was ah boy too, a'lil negro boy runnin wit Abram. He was out yonder close by the tall trees."

Their conversation was cut short by two men approaching swiftly yelling at them, "Medic!"

Lieutenant Goldman's voice was like a bullhorn. The Colonel and Scott both directed their attention towards the outburst. Behind the shouting man was Bushrod, clothes all torn, lump on the side of his forehead from his clumsy fall while waving the white flag.

"This is Scott, Mr. Collins's son. His pa' owner this plantation and now it's his."

Lieutenant Goldman started to explain that some of his men found two bodies closer to the treeline one wench and a nigger man. "The ole wench neck was damn near snapped in half. Are you the Colonel around here?"

Colonel Hitch replied, "Yes sur, I am. I handle the slaves here along with timber hauling, up by the swamps. Could you show me where these bodies are Lieutenant?"

Lieutenant Goldman helped Colonel Hitch to his feet.

"I'll be back Scott, sit tight now."

They talked as they walked towards the suspicious murder scene.

"One slave did all this Colonel?" Lieutenant Goldman asked.

The colonel looked at him briefly before turning back forward, "There's this nigga named Abram. Always thought something was funny bout em'. Always thought the nigga was one of dem reading niggers, neva thought he be brave enough to try something as evil as this, especially not alone."

Lieutenant Goldman interrupted, "Don't look like he alone sur. Seems he has some type of help from the looks of the escape route."

Lieutenant Goldman pointed at the blood trail lowering his lamp to the ground. "You know those dead mutts over there Colonel?"

The colonel was shocked to see Simon and Lydia lifeless on the ground. "This one here was Mr. Collins boss nigga, the wench was his...well, she was a lot of things to him."

Lieutenant shook his head with disgust. "Looks like she took a shot at someone around here that flintlock is still warm."

Lieutenant was doing a bit of detective work as Colonel Hitch just seem confused and angered. He was ready to kill.

"My militia has the hounds accompanied by the finest of sharpshooters. We'll track em down in no time Colonel don't you worry," Lieutenant Goldman grabbed his shoulder before mounting up.

Colonel Hitch responded, "And the boy?"

Lieutenant Goldman looked over at what was left of the house, "I'm leaving a small regiment of soldiers behind for safeguard. Until we catch this brutal, savage murderer, we have to secure this zone along with the property of a dead man."

"Understood," Colonel Hitch's hands were cold. He blew into them as he began to examine more of the area. He saw the gunpowder trails and horse tracks going in the direction of the woods.

Then there it was, looked like a small piece of paper under the dirt.Colonel Hitch picked it up it was bible paper with letters circled.

"Hemlock," Colonel Hitch dusted the page off and put it in his pants pocket. "May God help us all,"

Colonel Hitch knew at that moment Abram had not only did this but he has some serious help with the natives. The thought of an African and Native alliance brought chills to his spine. This was more strategic than expected. Especially with him being a deserter. He knew from the time he spent living in the swamp, how tactical the negroes and natives could be together and that he and Lieutenant Goldman really needed to be aware of what they were up against. However, he couldn't blow his cover or risk revealing he was in the dismal swamp. They could send him to military prison as a disgraceful cowardly soldier. He decided to keep quiet.

"Lieutenant Goldman let's move out!"

The hounds were barking, the soldiers were bloodthirsty, eyes wide under the moonlight. The hunt was active, now the hunt shall be.

ABOUT THE AUTHOR

Derek Godwin, aka, OACE al Mansur, spends most of his time in North Carolina, living a holistic vegan lifestyle for the past 5 years. He now operates Supreme being, a wellness business that he developed out of his own existence actively promoting healthy living. OACE Al Mansur continues his passion to write his revolutionized philosophy based on true events.

Be sure to visit his website:
 www.mysupremewellbeing.com
and join the email list.

www.ingramcontent.com/pod-product-compliance
Lightning Source LLC
Chambersburg PA
CBHW050128030726
47505CB00007B/2088